A Wolverine Lumberjack

A Wolverine Lumberjack

Mason Ray

Copyright © 2015 by Mason Ray.

ISBN: Softcover   978-1-5035-7719-0
        eBook   978-1-5035-7718-3

All rights reserved. No part of this book may be reproduced or transmitted in any form or by any means, electronic or mechanical, including photocopying, recording, or by any information storage and retrieval system, without permission in writing from the copyright owner.

This is a work of fiction. Names, characters, places and incidents either are the product of the author's imagination or are used fictitiously, and any resemblance to any actual persons, living or dead, events, or locales is entirely coincidental.

Any people depicted in stock imagery provided by Thinkstock are models, and such images are being used for illustrative purposes only.
Certain stock imagery © Thinkstock.

Print information available on the last page.

Rev. date: 07/20/2015

To order additional copies of this book, contact:
Xlibris
1-888-795-4274
www.Xlibris.com
Orders@Xlibris.com
713810

Contents

I	The Man of Mystery	1
II	Madeline Brett	13
III	Blair's Mill and Its Owner	23
IV	The Triple Terror of District Number Four	37
V	The Ginseng Diggers	45
VI	Spiked Logs at Blair's Mill	57
VII	Where is Donald Brett?	69
VIII	A Country Ball	81
IX	Madeline Brett Finds Employment	93
X	A District School	105
XI	A District School Riot	119
XII	The Search for Phil	129
XIII	The Quilting Bee	139
XIV	Making Maple Sugar	149
XV	What Bob Stray Found	159
XVI	Why Mann Learned to Swim	169
XVII	India Blair's Suitors	181
XVIII	The Fire	191

XIX	Bob Remembers	201
XX	A Gun Wedding	213
XXI	A Telepathic Message	229
XXII	Frosted Cakes	239

To the gallant army of lumberjacks who have cleared the way to civilization this book is respectfully dedicated.

E. Mason Ray
Glen Arbor, Michigan

I

The Man of Mystery

Slowly great flakes of early snow settled on the hill-ranges that billow away from Lake Superior to the shallow waters of Lake Erie, and from the "Thumb" on the east to the mammoth sand dunes on the west of Michigan. Through this smother of snow plodded the Hickory Vale to Agache stage with its one passenger. Joe Swanson, the Dane driver, flicked the dilatory buckskin with his rawhide whip, but the mustang, splotched on his side with patches of white, moved nervously and irritably bit at his mate's low hung nose and bridle.

Occasionally the old stage driver addressed the stranger in his soft dialect, naming the owners of forest sections or the scattered cabins, mainly log-built, that slipped by like bulky ghosts in the white silence. Twice they crossed darkly flowing streams, once they skirted the shore of a lake that heaved with dead swells as if the black water was half congealed.

"You bane here before?" questioned Joe, whose many years of driving engendered a keen interest in his passengers' affairs.

"No," admitted the traveler. His tone discouraged advances, but Joe persisted.

"Where bane your home, de udder place you live?"

During an astonishing long pause the stranger hesitated. Blue eyes that shaded to black were lowered in thought. Finally, like one who recalls an elusive name, he answered in a word.

"Manistee."

"What you want here anyways?" pursued his inquisitor. "Dere's nodding but mills, lumbermans and logs."

"I'm a lumberman, too," stated Joe's passenger. "A scaler. I'm to scale logs for Steel and Hawley."

Joe whistled as an escape valve for his astonishment.

"So," said he, "you're the scaler what comes in place of dat Thompson da boys run out!"

Silently the stage driver cogitated this interesting news while an Indian with a gun on his shoulder became a blurry shape, grew distinct and slouched by with his dog at heel.

"Dat's Shawnoga after rabbits," volunteered the driver. "He's from de Injun camp on de sout' shore of Muskrat Lake. It's nigh Steel and Hawley's beeg mill. Dat's a mill what is a mill – twenty gang saws running night and day soon's de ice breaks so's logs can be rafted. Dey should run all winter like dat udder ob Blair's, only Blair gets logs wit' teams right out de woods. Steel and Hawley should own bot' mills since they cut logs for bot' mills. You'll be keep busy. Nobody loafs what tally for eighty men."

Joe let this information adjust itself in his listener's brain while he urged his lagging team with horse talk the buckskin ignored and the mustang took to heart and heel for he bit his mate into a swinging trot. Presently a side road, a little better than a trail, appeared at their left.

"Dat bane a short cut to Steel and Hawley's camp," explained Joe. "I go t'ree miles udder way by Nuveen's store."

"Then I'll cut across," said the passenger.

"But your trunk," reminded Joe. "What name'll I tell Hicks who drives for camp supplies an' gets de camp mail?"

Again the stranger paused an amazing time before answering the simple query.

"The name's on my trunk," he finally told Swanson as if waking from a reverie. "It's easy to remember – just Mann, Forrest Mann, and the initials on my trunk are F.M."

Immediately Forrest Mann placed the amount of his fare in Joe's unmittened hand, leaped to the untrodden snow and swung with a vigorous stride into the half-obliterated trail. On either hand gray tree trunks upheld a dome of leafless branches like the columns of some vast temple floored in white. Everywhere was a silence so profound that the chattering of a squirrel seemed unnaturally loud. It was a place suited to hooded monks, white-surpliced choir boys or black-robed nuns. Impelled by this nameless majesty of the forest the traveler stopped a moment with cap lifted, gazing into the depth of the wilderness.

Standing thus he was himself an object worthy of notice. Like the timber about him he was straight and tall and powerful. His strong, handsome features indicated depth of character. The dark blue eyes were open and frank, and above the high forehead nut-brown hair rolled back in a crisp wave. His heavy mustache half concealed a sensitive mouth. His chin was firm and his eyes had a trick of smiling.

Before long the self-named traveler emerged in a slashing where the distant thud of ax-blows ended in the thunder of down-crashing timber. At the left of this brush-littered area he saw the long, low buildings of Steel and Hawley's lumbering camp. Snow had ceased to fall. Late November twilight wrapped the primitive scene in dull gray atmosphere that made necessary the lamp light now yellowing the camp's small paned windows. Mann followed a path past the slab-roofed barn, opened the battened door of the bunk-house and entered a room sixty feet in length by twenty five in width. Along each side were double rows of bunks, straw-filled and blanketed. At the exact center of the oblong space there glowed a square-sided fireplace, built to give warmth to the greatest number, and smoke-drained by a stick-made chimney with protruding ends.

Standing by it with his long arms full of wood he was about to fling on the blaze was Guy, the camp chore boy. This sudden advent of a stranger paralyzed him into a grotesque figure. With heavy red head a-tilt, his porcine eyes blinking and his loose mouth showing red gums in a wide grin he stood apparently unable to move.

"Let me help," offered the newcomer, and tossed Guy's maple wood on coals that promptly sent a shower of sparks. This unlooked for assistance had the unfortunate effect of nearly toppling Guy into the fire after his burden, but, recovering his balance by a whirl of his abnormal arms, he stood grinning and nodding from excess bashfulness.

"Good evening," said the new scaler in tardy greeting. "What's your name?"

"G' – Guy," slobbered the boy in an ecstasy of confusion.

"Where's the boss?"

"C' – comin'," stuttered Guy.

"All right, Guy, I'll wait for him. I'm expected."

With another whirl of arms, this time to give impetus, Guy departed, swaying from side to side and deeply nodding, by way of a door toward the cook house just as the bunk-room door swung wide to three teamsters and a rush of cold air.

"Blast a country that don't know its own mind," grouched the treble tones of Watson, a thick-set, curly haired man of abbreviated stature.

"Hoot, mon, this is naught but a flurry," retorted big McManus who dressed in a near substitute for Highland plaid – the gay mackinaw coat of the lumberjack. "Who's yon by the fire?" he added in a low mumble.

The man he addressed was a six-footer named Dan Hilliker who slapped loose snow from his cap before hanging it on a peg. "Like's not it's the new scaler," said he. "Brett and Brinkley's looking for him."

"Lord have mercy on him," muttered Watson, "if he's another sucker."

"You're hogging that broom, Watson," objected Hilliker, standing with snow-crusted feet apart and his red and green mackinaw open at the throat exposing a brawny chest.

"Take it," offered the curly headed teamster with a fling of the article in question which Hilliker caught and began to ply on his boots. Presently the trio, with impersonal nods of greeting, joined Mann at the fire where benches formed a square. Each man instantly dived into a rear pocket and produced a pipe and tobacco and, having deftly filled the pipes, stooped to the fire and adroitly lighted up with coals that set the tobacco glowing and filled the air with curling smoke.

"Does Mr. Brett, the manager, stop here at the camp?" The question was impartially addressed to the three by Forrest Mann, but McManus answered.

"Brett lives on his farm and gang's round by the road, but Brinkley will show you the w'y by lantern. It's a mile or so yon," said the Scotchman, pointing the direction with his pipe.

As he spoke the outer door crashed inward to admit group after group of sawyers, choppers, top-loaders, road-monkeys and late teamsters all wearing the universal plaid mackinaw. The shifting, jostling, joking, grumbling crowd displayed in their garbs every tint of the rainbow and some colors not included in the spectrum. Chaffing, loud laughter, friendly scuffing, demands for tobacco and lights formed a sound medley characteristic of lumber crews in the tall timber at quitting time. With a thrill of admiration Mann watched the milling about of sturdy forms, graceful and free as the wind-driven sweep of bending pines.

"Tat's a tam pig snow for log-cut," piped the shrill voice of Jules Deveraux, a Canadian Frenchman.

"You hain't no need to growl," observed Jim Sprik. "When you grab the lines over them blacks you won't know whether it's snowing or fog. They'll yank you between the flakes. Black lightening, them hosses."

Instant laughter applauded the witticism. The blacks, King and Queen, were a pair of untamed devils in horse flesh; and, in that pioneer region of slow-moving ox teams few lumberjacks wanted to drive mettlesome steeds.

"By gar," shouted the quick-tempered Frenchman, "I pet what you lak dat I win! I'll drive dat team or bus'."

"Then you'll bus', Frenchy," predicted a voice as the door screeched open to admit a tall, dark-featured man whose alert eyes instantly singled out the stranger by the fire. He strode forward and with abrupt heartiness grasped Mann's extended hand. His manner was almost boisterously genial.

"I'm Brinkley, the foreman," he explained in full lunged tones. "And of course you're the tally man expected by Brett. How'd you get here? Stage?"

Mann related his manner of arrival, then said, "I expected to see Mr. Brett at once and receive orders."

"No hurry about orders," cried Brinkley in his hearty, loud toned manner, the tone of a man who speaks his mind regardless of listeners. "We'll feed first then I'll take you over to Brett's. The former scaler kept a room there for the sake of his books, but he ate here and you'll likely fare the same."

As Brinkley conversed with the new scaler men surged about the stick fireplace and hung every sort of socks and mitten on the uneven ends to dry. Many poles soon took on a motely array in every color and looked, as Jim Sprik remarked, like a square deal Christmas tree.

"You misname it," laughed a big Irishman named Munshaw. "It's a pear tree – pairs of mittens and socks, by hokey."

Above the roar that bellowed out at Munshaw's pun Brinkley shouted a command. "Boys, here's Mr. Mann, your new scaler! Give him a lumberjack's welcome."

There ensued a moment's silence, a waiting silence. Then McManus rose to his feet and led a cheer that made the room vibrate. Again the cheer was repeated by eighty lusty voices, and a third time their: "What's the matter with Mr. Mann? Oh, he's all right!" held a significant emphasis. As its vigor rattled the windows Long Jim, the cook, rushed from the adjoining shanty, thrust his black head around the edge of the partly open door and suspiciously eyed the noisy woodsmen.

"See here," he shouted. "If you galoots air hinting for supper you can change your tune. I ain't going to hustle for nobody. Not if you yell your damn heads off." He glared at the offending company but as his lengthy nose had been broken and favored his left ear, the glare became whimsical drollery that sent the lumberjacks off in a volley of cheers for "Long Jim." This was a tribute, not a grouch. So as Jim's outstanding ears caught good-natured variations of his name he became mollified and added a grudging invitation.

"Seeing as the grub's ready and hot," he yelled, "you might's well come 'long to the cook house an' fill your mouths with something healthier 'en a gol darn racket." At that he withdrew, turtle-wise, and disappeared.

Instantly the room emptied in his wake. Lumber jacks surged across the trampled space between the shanties and settled about two long tables in Jim's cook room. Mann, escorted by Brinkley, was seated at the end of one of the oil-cloth covered boards now loaded with an abundance of fried pork, beans, bread, cookies, dried apple pie, and tin cups of boiling hot tea. Profound silence prevailed. This was the hour lumberjacks fed without words, giving full attention to the business in hand. After hunger was subsided one and another called jocular remarks to Guy who, with heavy head bobbing and body swaying, replenished plates with a celerity that belied his shambling gait.

"Come, Guy, hustle them beans before they sprout," urged Bill Watson's shrill treble.

"'Tain't the beans what's sprouting. It's Guy," guffawed Ben Heald. The general laugh increased Guy's stumbling and widened his red mouth grin, but he evidently enjoyed the jest.

"Don't talk beans to Guy," spoke up a thin, querulous voice. "He don't know beans. "The speaker was a lean, stoop-shouldered man whose pinched features reminded Mann of a bird of prey. His eyes were shifty and half concealed by lowered head and bushy brows. Ominous quiet followed his coarse jest. Guy, despite his awkwardness, was a camp favorite. His doddering form and wide grinning mouth was to them a cheerful sight therefore he had many friends and one of them now voiced his opinion.

"Sacre!" blazed Jules Deveraux. "Dat's a tam lie."

The Frenchman's remark was addressed to a young man at his right. The youth was slender, refined in appearance and retiring in manner. His serious brown eyes seldom lifted, but when Mann encountered the lad's glance he was impressed by something indefinably strange in the youth's expression. Although the delicate features showed good birth and intelligence he looked like one lost and bewildered.

"That," said Brinkley, noting the scaler's interest in the lad, "is a chap who came to us two years ago. He has worked about the mill and camp ever since. We call him Bob Stray since no one, including himself, has the least glimmering of his name or home."

Mann studied the cameo-fine countenance, and elusive as a will-o'-the-wisp, was the sensation that somewhere at some time he had before been face to face with Bob Stray. The scaler's handsome features paled at the thought and his lowered eyes were troubled pools until he was rouse to the present by abruptly moving lumberjacks whose wolfish appetites were cloyed. One by one they flung their feet over the long bench and returned to the bunk-room with its kerosene lights and roaring fire. Belated teamsters were warming their chilled fingers before crossing to the cook shanty for supper.

"Well, Chet," Brinkley called to the nearest, "how's the going?"

"It's a confounded mess," Chet Brooks told the boss. "We hardly banked a thousand each."

"Never mind," encouraged Brinkley. "You'll see a month of Injun summer yet. Just keep 'em moving. Steel and Hawley want the biggest rollways ever banked on Muskrat Lake. They want a record breaker and every log helps." The foreman spoke in his manner of good-fellowship. He had the rare gift of magnetism that drew men to him and gave him control over them. Hearty, intimate kindness marked his most trivial utterance. Brinkley was a master of men.

"Now for Brett's," he told the tally man. "Wait till I light a lantern. The night's thick as blackstrap and twice as dark."

While the foreman applied a match to his lantern the door screeched open to admit a gaunt individual whose great height was absurdly out of proportion to his bony frame. Humorous eyes twinkled in his lean, lightly bearded face. His garb was the regulation mackinaw, heavy trousers and cloth cap. Over his shoulder was swung the bag of clothing lumberjacks called a turkey and, to Mann's amazement, a huge tortoise-shell cat was cuddled under his arm.

"Hello, Brinkley," said the man in a voice that rose and fell in cheerful squeaks. "I'm looking for a job, by gol. An' I say," he interceded, "I 'spose you don't mind m' cat. Tam's my family. He's all the folks I got."

"I shan't object if the cook don't," laughed Brinkley. "But I ain't anxious to have cats the style. One ain't bad but eighty 'u'd be worse 'en horse fiddles. As for work, hang up your hat."

"That's the best top-loader in the state," Brinkley told Mann when they were on their way. "And top-loading is 'bout as safe as squinting down a gun barrel with the trigger set. That's why Haywire Hank's welcome, cat or no cat."

For a time the two men walked briskly along the white trail in the lantern's glow. Moss grown tree trunks appeared to march by them in stately phalanx. Suddenly above them sounded the blood curdling call of a screech owl, and from the distant murk came the answering cry.

"Hear that?" cried Brinkley who strode ahead. "Them pop-eyed critters are hollering for rain – or mischief."

II

Madeline Brett

The commodious, log-built home of Donald Brett, manager of the Steel and Hawley lumbering interests, set in an expanse of snow that bent evergreens to the earth and capped stumps in unrecognizable forms. Even the log walls were dusted with crystal and window panes were outlined with white. Circling the clearing was a rim of forest that extended miles southward, while in a westerly direction the wilderness opened to make room for Muskrat Lake.

Within the manager's humble dwelling was luxurious comfort. The red-tinted walls of the large front room gave no hint of logs beneath smooth plaster. Rich hangings, a deep piled rug, a well filled bookcase, easy chairs, a couch and an old style piano made a suitable environment for the one woman present. Madeline Brett, who watched the storm from a window, revealed a profile of exquisite outline. Her pale olive skin contrasted with high combed raven black hair, expressive eyes like midnight pools, and eyebrows black as ink.

"Donald, are you going to camp?" she questioned without removing her gaze from the snow-veiled forest.

The other occupant of the room, Donald Brett, enjoyed the prime of life. His strong featured face, large head, thick set form, unresponsive gray eyes and masked expression indicated a stoic character. He sat reading before a wood fire, feet on the fender and smoke rings from his pipe curling above the printed sheet. For all of his wife's query, he was stolidly silent. She was not disturbed for this man of Scotch ancestry was habitually chary of speech and typically reticent.

"Donald, are you going to camp?" Madeline Brett's liquid utterance repeated the question as one drop succeeds another in the slow wearing away of rock.

"Yes," said Brett finally. Then as if one word paved the way for others he added, "Hawley wrote that I might expect the new scaler today. He's to stop here nights. Have Sally prepare Thompson's room."

"Coming – in this storm!" exclaimed Mrs. Brett, roused from her abstraction. "Where is he from?"

The manager made no addition to his first statement. He rose deliberately, knocked the ash from his pipe into the glowing grate then passed out to the kitchen at the rear and directed Sam, the hired man, to harness his team. Presently, fur-coated and buried in robes, he started on his rounds which included the camp and later, the store that supplied provisions for Steel and Hawley's lumberjacks.

After her husband's departure Madeline drew her chair to the fire, placed her daintily slippered feet on the fender lately used by Brett, and thought of the stranger who was to share their home. Was he young or old, attractive or repellent? Would he be offensive like Thompson? She recalled the former tally man with unspeakable loathing, but Brett was undisturbed. That her fastidious sense was daily outraged by the man's presence mattered nothing to the manager. Thompson was a useful and necessary tool, therefore to be endured. At last lumbermen, because of Thompson's trickery, refused his scale and Brett, himself the soul of honor, sent on to Hawley for another scaler. Madeline rejoiced. The departure of Thompson left the atmosphere clean. But another was coming that night. Would he be an improvement, or a pest?

The mistress of the log bungalow had lived a sheltered life. She had experienced but one deep sorrow. Five years before an infant son had briefly visited the Brett household. When it died Madeline's grief burned away her youth. She had lost nature's best gift and it left her spiritually dead. Brett, however, seemed to forget the happening and supposed – if he gave the matter any thought – that his wife's memory of the distressing event was likewise dulled. But to her starved mother heart the child's individuality was real and his growth kept pace with the years. She began to think of him as her delicate fingers wove lace with an ivory hook. He would be a lively lad in boyish suits learning at her knee, a constant companion and probably a trouble maker for old Sally. Her vividly red lips smiled. Then a tangle demanded attention. As she stared at the pretty trifle in her strong, flexible fingers her thoughts took a new direction.

"Is this my life's accomplishment?" she pondered with disgust. "Do I exist for no better purpose?"

Like one rousing from hypnosis she fixedly gazed at the thing which, toher, represented her mature womanhood. She had drifted into idleness of brain and body, becoming atrophied for want of economic interests.

"I am a living death," she mused angrily. "Have I existed a quarter of a century for this?"

Without hesitation she unraveled the useless fabric to its commencement and wound the thread on the half emptied spool. The act was her answer. And, having destroyed the symbol of her squandered past, she stepped to a bookcase and removed several volumes from a lower shelf which she placed on a baize-covered table together with pencil and notebook. Her dark head bent above a tome which she read absorbedly until she forgot time and place. This study was Madeline's secret diversion – a world of strange delight and promise. It was knowledge for which she hungered and thirsted. Because of an irresistible inclination inherited form her physician father and a line of the same school before him, she craved an understanding of disease and it alleviation. This curious inheritance was as natural as an instinct for music. But, because Brett bitterly opposed what he called an abnormal taste, she was forced to clandestine draughts at the forbidden fount.

Upon this occasion she pursued her amazing recreation until late in the afternoon when Sam's wife appeared in the doorway like a crayon sketch and voiced an announcement.

"Miss Liney, har's Mis' Swisher. She's outen de kitchen waitin' to see yo', honey."

Madeline looked up and smiled at the fat Negress who had followed her fortune from Virginia to that wild region, and dragged with her a reluctant spouse. Both Negroes were old family servants and their devotion to "Miss Liney" was that of parents to a beloved daughter. To Madeline they represented home in a true sense. Because of her southern training they were almost necessary to her happiness, and she was willing to permit Sally dominant sway in the kitchen, nor dreamed of distressing the capable Negress by usurping her rights.

"Coming, Aunt Sally," she said in her sweet contralto that was as mellow as Sally's own dialect. She was not surprised that Mrs. Swisher had braved the inclement weather nor that the caller insisted upon remaining in the rear room. Settlement neighbors invariably circled the house until they found a kitchen entrance. The handsome front room seemed to afflict them with mental paralysis although it would require more that ornamental rugs to paralyze Mrs. Swisher's razor wit.

"I just run in a minute, Mis' Brett," said the caller in crisp swift utterance. She was an elderly woman with twinkling black eyes, good humored face, pudgy form and the abrupt movements of a wren. "I told Sarah, says I," she continued breathlessly, "that I was going to the post office and call at Brett's. Says I, I'm going to git out while I'm living for I'll likely be a long time dead."

"I'm glad you came," Madeline assured her heartily. "Besides, it can't be very cold or the snow would be powdery instead of wet."

"It's soft as mush," declared Mrs. Swisher. "Tomorrow the hull country will be naked as a plucked goose which'll suit the loggers. As for me I don't care a d--, I mean a cuss whether the land's black or white. The more the men earn the more they shove across Bender's bar for his devilish whiskey. An' there's that gambling hole o' Sacket's where the men play poker till God's sun puts out the lamps. Them halfwit gamblers 'u'd play on their wives' coffins with coppers that shut down their poor dead eyelids. I know 'em. Swisher can't fool me. It'll be a cold day 'fore he shuts my eyes with coppers or anything else. As for my mouth he can't shut that a-tall. I tells him what I thinks. Once when he played all night I told him I wished to God lightening 'u'd strike at the table. Well, you know Swisher. Nothing jolts him. He's too slow to catch measles or the grace of God at Brother Johnathan's revival. Says he, 'Lightening wouldn't have any effect on that crowd, Maria. They're tougher 'en oak knots.'"

Mrs. Swisher delivered her caustic remarks with the utmost sprightliness. Like country dwellers she was interested in local dissipations and general happenings, also she was shrewdly aware that her report of Bender and Sacket's hanging out places were unvarnished truth and that many poverty stricken households had bitter cause to rail at lawless conditions.

"If the men all lose at poker, who gains?" asked Madeline.

"Nordyke," snapped Mrs. Swisher. "He ain't content to grind the man on wages and double their store bills for chuck, but on top o' that he takes a hand at cards and pockets the poor fools' cash."

"How can Nordyke limit wages?" inquired Madeline. "He's only the firm's bookkeeper."

"Mis' Brett, you're the manager's wife, but just the same I'll tell you what everybody knows. Nordyke's the real power. Don't he hire and fire and never ask

Brett? Ain't he the one who handles every cent of the firm's cash for wages and timber? Didn't he do his best to keep track on that sneak of a Thompson until men selling logs threatened tar and feathers?"

"I know nothing about business affairs," confessed Madeline. "Mr. Brett never mentions his work or his worries."

"Mr. Brett is all right," proclaimed her caller. "You oughta hear what he's called in camp. Them lumberjacks 'u'd name the saints and they call Brett 'Square-sill' which means the same as honest."

"I'm glad Donald's nickname is so complimentary," laughed his wife who stood by Sally's table preparing a plate of cake and pouring a cup of hot chocolate for her guest.

"Don't you bother," remonstrated Mrs. Swisher, but she drank the steaming beverage and ate the cake which turned her attention to the cook.

"What you making, Sally?" she sociably inquired.

"Gingerbread fo' supper," said Sally, and whisked her batter with renewed energy.

"One egg, or two?"

"Two," said the cook. "But w'en the hens don' lay I c'n git 'long outen any."

"Come to meeting Sunday night and hear the Quaker woman," invited Mrs. Swisher as she finished her lunch and rose to go. "She's sent here from Indiana to convert the heathen, and for one I wish her luck. So far's I'm concerned nobody could give me religion that 'u'd last over pay day. Pay day means poker an' I get so blazing mad it most sets my hair afire. Anyhow, come and hear her."

The caller bustled out, shut the door behind her with a snap and proceeded on her way to Nuveen's store where neighbors met as at a club to exchange gossip. After her departure Madeline spread the dining table, at one end of the big kitchen, with snowy linen, adding dainty china, glass and silver that had been wedding presents, then invaded the pantry in search of edibles.

"Now, Miss Liney, honey, don' yo' mess wid vittles," objected Sally who was beating waffles for the coming meal.

"I must do something or I'll die of inaction," declared her mistress. "I'll become as idle as an oyster."

"Nebber yet saw anybody die o' laziness," scoffed Sally. "If laziness kills folks, my Sam 'u'd been dead afore I ebber see him."

The sound of Brett's team passing to the barn warned the cook it was time to heat her waffle irons and hasten the hot cakes. Before long the manager seated himself opposite Madeline at the bountiful board. He approvingly noted favorite dishes that were an achievement of one of the old South's best cooks.

"Hal Roth's family lost a child last night," he remarked as he dismembered a roast chicken. The news was volunteered with unusual freedom. Good food and warm fires after a day in the open induced genial speech even if the theme lacked cheer. His wife's dark eyes mutely questioned. "Pneumonia probably," he added. "These country people are at sea when a cold goes wrong. Their medical ability begins and ends with rheumatism and ague."

After this sociability Brett settled to silent enjoyment of his evening dinner, but Madeline's thoughts were with the unfortunate Roth family.

"The mother didn't know how to save her child. Like myself she was ignorant until too late. If I had been with her, I might have been of use."

Bitterly she rebelled against Brett's opposition to her giving medical advice and aid to settlement families. The urge of life-saving generations would have drawn her to bedsides where simple remedies might prevail, but her husband loathed a woman practitioner and was morbidly jealous of what he called her unfortunate heritage; so he coldly forbade her to exercise the unwomanly gift and Brett's will was law.

A clock on the bookcase neared the hour of eight when heavy steps on the porch heralded the arrival of the boss, Brinkley, and the new scaler. Then the door swung open on a square of night revealing Brinkley and the man who was to remain with the manager's household.

"Here's your log-reckoner, Brett," was the foreman's introduction. "Fetched him over, but guess I'll hike back and get some sleep. Them teamsters quarrel like bobcats over first place in the morning. I have to be up and settle 'em. Good night."

By the time her husband formally presented the scaler by name, Madeline had decided in his favor. His manner showed breeding, refinement. She was relieved. Her chilling reserve became cordial greeting.

"You're in the heart of the wilderness, Mr. Mann," she smiled. "I hope you enjoy solitude."

"If not there are compensations," said the scaler with a glance about the book-lined, glowing room. "A book takes you anywhere."

Brett began to talk business.

"You're employed here in a double capacity," he informed the tally man. "Steel and Hawley not only bank logs for their summer's cut, but cut and haul logs for the Blair mill. You scale for both firms although Blair confirms the scale. Saturday of each week you report to Blair and the Steel and Hawley bookkeeper. A supply team will take you out and back."

As the men talked Madeline sat in a cozy-hollow chair that engulfed her slender form. The satin of her olive skin was flushed as a flame glows through alabaster, and her large dark eyes flashed with unusual animation. She was thinking of her girlhood in old Virginia.

"Where is your residence?" the manager asked his scaler. "I know you now came from Manistee. Is that your home?"

Madeline, too, waited for the answer, but it was delayed. One might have thought Forrest Mann had not heard until he replied in a low voice, "I'm something of a wanderer. There is no spot that I may claim as home."

Brett accepted this as a touch of his own reticence, and settled back into a smoke-enveloped reverie.

When the newly arrived tally-man retired to Thompson's former room his mind was a whirl of undulating forest, half frozen lakes, a lumber camp and its inmates; but clearer than all was the beautiful face of Madeline Brett.

III

Blair's Mill and Its Owner

Forrest Mann, clad in a gray mackinaw, corduroy trousers and high spiked boots, might have posed as a typical knight of the timber lands. Nor were the crusaders better employed than the stalwart army who opened the way to civilization with saw and ax. About him in the doomed forest twanged the saw-requiem of giant pines and lordly maples. In every direction the woods was veined with new roads that converged with the main highway. At intervals along these branches were piles of logs on skids which Mann was to scale and direct his assistant to stamp with the company's symbol of 'S.H.' or Blair's 'B.'—raised letters on a steel maul. The assistant selected by Brinkley to accompany the scaler was Bob Stray. Brett himself instructed Mann in his day's work.

"These skidways north of the road," he explained, "are Blair's. Steel and Hawley purchased a section of the Blair timber, and we pay in delivered logs. Stamp them accordingly and rush the tally. We're behind."

"Here's where we put our mark on the Blair's logs," Mann told the lad with the forgotten past.

"All right. I can do it," Bob Stray assured him. "I've done it before because I stamped logs for Thompson." His gentle, eager eyes were raised to Mann's face with the usual wistful expression of one groping for memory. Mann's heart ached with compassion, and Bob found a loyal, sympathetic friend, a friend who furthered his interests without regard to his own.

Near them Hilliker and Haywire Hank bit canthooks into the ends of a huge elm log that was to cap the skidway while the placid oxen chewed cud and awaited developments. Brinkley watched the performance and yelled orders.

"Now, boys, hook 'er up," he shouted. "Look out! That there end is sluing! Quick!"

By a margin the log missed the pinnacle and rolled back almost to the heels of the skidding team.

"Judas Priest!" squeaked Haywire Hank. "Them cattle's born lucky."

"So was you," stormed Hilliker. "If you ain't saved for hanging you'd be dead."

While Mann deftly applied his rule to log ends, jotted down the result in his tally book and signaled Bob to swing his sledge, he became aware that he was wolfishly hungry. He had eaten heartily of Long Jim's flapjacks that morning, so his condition astonished him and he expressed his amazement to Bob.

"By noon," said Bob, "you'll eat beans by the quart and wish each one was the size of a potato."

Mann laughed. Then he became aware that his assistant had lapsed into his waking dream with fixed gaze like one studying the answer to a perplexing query.

"What are you thinking about, Bob?"

"Potatoes," said the boy. "I was trying to remember when I first saw potatoes. I am always trying to remember. I try to think where I belong, where I came from. Seems as if a word – my name or home town – would unravel the snarl."

Mann looked pityingly at the familiar features. "If your name is ordinary," he suggested, "you must hear it often or see it in print."

"I've listened close," said Bob regretfully, "but my name must be unusual for I never hear it. As for print, my knowledge of that went too. I'm trying to learn to read but it's slow work."

"Let me help," offered Mann. "Mrs. Brett won't mind if you study in my room. An hour evenings will turn the trick. What do you say?"

"I say it's a grand chance," ejaculated Bob with eyes shining. "But I can't have you bothered. It's too much to ask."

"Never mind that. It's a bargain," declared Mann. Again he studied the young victim of amnesia, but the face would not fit into a niche of time and place. He was forced to decide Bob merely resembled a former acquaintance. Whatever the truth he would not hesitate in helping Bob to his memory even if it caused his own undoing.

The remaining half week slipped rapidly into the last working day, the day Mann was to accompany the supply team to Blair's mill and report the 'B.' tally before going to the Company's store where the 'S.H.' scale was turned in to the firm's bookkeeper. His trip was made with Jules Deveraux and his fractious team of blacks. As they drove through the chopping, Paul

Duff and Jack Winters, standing on either side of a huge pine, sent practiced ax-blades to its heart. Dizzily the quivering tree whirled on its base as the choppers shouted the familiar warning of "Timber!" and ran to safety. Slowly the monarch settled toward the deeper gash in its side and rushed downward, landing with a reverberating crash. Immediately Mike Munshaw and Moss Higbee appeared with a crosscut saw, and the high-pitched, musical chime of the deep-toothed blade followed Mann as the nervous blacks darted past the danger zone.

"Steety now," admonished Jules. "Tat's fuss rate. Hol' on, Queen, you debbil. Dere, tat's bully. Now King, you lazy peast, keep up. By gar, I'll show you!" he yelled while flicking his whip. "Ho's tat? On wiz you. Sacre, tat's one gran' trot."

It was. King and Queen dashed along the forest-walled road to Muskrat Lake like harnessed whirlwinds. Southward miles of timbered hills and vales rolled away like a storm tossed sea, but Steel and Hawley's choppings disfigured the right. Then the forest avenue abruptly ended at a hill's crest and before them lay a panorama in grays of the Blair buildings and the slow heaving water of Muskrat Lake, rimmed by hills – one of which was a giant sand dune at the extreme west.

"Over tat ridge is Lake Michigan," Jules shouted. "Agache where we go is py the shore." These words seemed blown form his lips as his team shot down the incline to the lake rollways where a teamster was unloading logs.

"Whip up them black cats," shrilled Watson whose curls out-rimmed his cap. "If you don't hustle you'll be late for Christmas.

"Dat so?" Jules yelled back. "Agache fuss rate place for stop. Heap skinawaubo at Benders." In sheer bravado he lashed each black whereupon they bolted past Mann's destination. "Jump," yelled Jules. "Tat's Blair's meel."

Mann precipitately obeyed. When he gained his feet Jules and the team were circling the lake road, but the Frenchman had control of his fiery steeds. The incident had an effect of dumping the scaler at the stranger's place of business and leaving him to find its owner – Blair.

For some rods Mann traversed a sawdust road among lumber and slab piles to the sawmill, fire-guarded along its ridge by sentinel water barrels that would be useless in mid-winter. At its rear was a mill pond covered with floating logs. By the mill he passed a sawdust chute disgorging its yellow stream that was the forest's life blood. Beyond the noisy engine room he entered the mill and ascended a short stair to the work floor above. Roaring machinery and screaming saws filled the place with sounds of bedlam. Therefore he stood unnoticed while he looked about for someone who might be Blair.

While he waited a huge maple log deliberately slid up the outside door slide on an endless chain and came to rest on the steam carriage. Instantly an iron "kicker" shunted it into place, and from the lower regions a mill worker bobbed up serenely and levered it into position for the saw. With his lean hand in the lever Bill Balsam stood by the circular blade of steel with deep-socketed grey eyes fixed on the advancing log. His spare frame, his eyes narrowed to the gaze of one deafened by years of screeching saws, his nervous hand guiding the whirling teeth into the doomed log made a study that riveted Mann's attention until a firm touch on his arm recalled him with a start to the present and his errand.

He turned to confront a young woman clad in a short skirted brown corduroy suit, with cap to match, and high laced boots of tan. Dark eyes gazed at him scrutinizing. The girl's strong features possessed a piquant witchery, and the full red lips curled in a half suppressed smile.

Motioning him to follow she preceded him down the stair and into the open away from deafening sounds. As she moved the scaler noted her swift light step, the girl's graceful carriage that told of outdoor living. Finally she turned with a laugh that revealed white teeth of perfect health.

"Pardon me for not speaking," she said in clear, decisive tones. "But my vocal power is not equal to that hubbub."

Mann lifted his hat in a delayed act of courtesy. "I'm the scaler acting for Steel and Hawley, also this mill. Will you please direct me where to find Blair, the owner?"

The girl's dark eyes widened in astonishment.

"I'm Blair," she said simply. "Weren't you told?"

Mann crimsoned. Why in Tophet hadn't Brett explained? Why hadn't anyone enlightened him? Could it be possible this girl had charge of a mill, commanded a mill crew? Miss Blair, considering her identity established, again signaled him to follow.

"I want you to examine one of Thomson's rollways," she told him. "The logs are a fraud, a cheat. I won't accept them. I've been waiting for you to come and rescale the whole lot."

Evidently Miss Blair had a temper. Again with firm, quick step she led the way to logs piles by a river; and into the tally-man's heart flooded the conviction that this imperious woman might beckon him to the world's end and he would gladly respond.

"See," she pointed, "what Thompson thought fit for Blair's mill." They were by an inlet to the lake where the Blair rollways waited for the saw. Mann stared at the lot with amazement. The timber was almost useless. "You see," she cried. "Do you think I'll pay for such logs – shakes, hollow-hearts, punkwood? Never! I want you to go over them and have the scale taken from my account."

The girl looked inquiringly at the Steel and Hawley scaler who was to decide the Blair gain or loss. She wondered what sort of a man the powerful firm had sent as a go-between. Was he honest? Would he be just and show neither fear nor favor? While the scaler appraised the condemned rollway his fine face darkened with anger at what he saw – logs blackened with rot, hollow with decay, whitened with punk.

"Thompson must have been mad," he commented with heat, "or a fool. No man in his senses would pass such stuff. It's worthless. If I had my timber rule with me," he began. But the relieved mill girl understood. Her weather tanned, piquant face brightened as his own darkened. She knew her cause was won.

"I'll get mine," she cut in. "I scale every stick that enters or leaves the yard. Wait!"

Leaving Mann standing by the river she hastened toward the smoke-pouring, noisy mill. Her movements were free and lithe as she passed direct over slabs and banked logs to a rear opening. Her grace was instinctive. She was entirely lacking in self-consciousness. Her mind was on the problem of forcing profit where the mill books had registered loss. She faced difficulties that might well test the sagacity of an experienced lumberman, and she was that, for India Blair knew timber and its manufacture from forest to dock.

As the new scaler jotted down figures form fraudulent rollways India enlightened him as to conditions.

"Thompson flatly refused to reconsider these log piles," she told Mann. "He was a scoundrel. No wonder the men made the woods too hot for him. They knew he was a plausible, fawning tool of the firm."

Mann worked silently while his companion closely observed each computation, but her practiced eye found nothing to condemn. When the last undesirable log was recorded in the scaler's notebook she suggested with a smile of gratitude, "Now we'll step over to my office and compare figures."

With this in view the two crossed the lumber yard, followed a narrow path that led over a rustic bridge spanning the river, and on to the Blair residence. It was an oddly planned building. The rear abutted on a high terrace while the main part dropped ten feet to a lower level. It reminded Mann of something seated on a ridge with feet on the ground watching the dead swells of Muskrat Lake. Their hard-trodden path ended at a side door of the elevated wing and they entered an office furnished with a roll-top desk, an iron safe and the further appointments of a comfortable library.

"Here's my back tally sheets," India said, producing them from a drawer in the desk. "And here's the scale of Thompson's cull logs." She pushed forward an arm chair for Mann's convenience as he compared three sets of figures – the one he had just completed, Blair's scale and Thompson's computation of the rejected timber.

"According to your tally I have short-scaled," said Mann finally looking up. "You gave them credit for every board that could be cut—and more."

India smiled. "Then the balance is in my favor. Steel and Hawley's tally-man never before showed an inclination to do us justice. Thank you."

They discussed the probable amount of the winter's cut before Mann rejoined his driver and the subdued blacks, and as Blair of Blair's mill talked she showed an intimate knowledge of every phase of lumbering. To the scaler she was a revelation. Her level gaze and crisp speech, her utter lack of self-consciousness impressed him strongly. She typified the great wilderness, wind-swept, clean, powerful. Most accurately she fitted into her environment of forest, lake and booming machine. Furthermore the name she signed to his accepted scale report – India Blair – preeminently suited her vigorous personality.

When Mann departed India watched the retreating figure of the stalwart lumberjack until a cedar hedge hid it from view, then she descended an open stairway to a lake view sitting room where an elderly woman with a sweet face and tranquil eyes sat sewing.

"Well, daughter?" The words were a question.

"Steel and Hawley's scaler is just and honest," India reported as she stooped to kiss the upturned face. "There's to be no more bad logs, mumma-mine. Even you, with your unshakable faith in human-kind, might safely deal with him."

"I'm glad," said Mrs. Blair thankfully. "I knew everything would come out right. You're a good manager, India, like your father. His judgement was sound. When he left you in control of the mill he knew you would succeed. Success is in the Blair blood. You can't fail."

Again India bent and kissed the sweet optimist. But she said nothing of men who quit her employ and had to be replaced, of slow payment for shipped lumber and unsettled debts. Blair had shielded his wife from bitterness of business troubles and the daughter followed his example. Not for worlds would she weaken her mother's belief in ultimate victory.

"Jules," questioned the scaler, again on his way, "why does Miss Blair run a lumber mill? Has she no relatives to fill the place?"

"No," Jules informed him. "W'en her dad was keel py de bust of a pig circular saw he say, 'India you run tat meel an' pay off de mortgage.' Blair, he know his girl is one leetle lumberjack. Ever since she so high," Jules illustrated with his whip, "she tags heem all round de woods and meel. She knows lumbering with her primer. So she do what Blair say and keep de hands busy. She sure one grand little lumberjack; dat so."

The mettlesome blacks soon skirted the south bluff and crossed the long narrows bridge, then trotted along the west shoulder of the larger lake to their destination at Agache. Agache straggled among pines each side of a highway that led to the Lake Michigan dock. It was the main street whose chief structure was the Company's long white store where Jules tied his team to a rope-girdled tree.

Within, the store was divided by a part-way partition which divided groceries from dry goods. Back of the grocery counter stood Redman, the head clerk who was dark, slim and active.

"You'll find Nordyke in the office," he told Mann, and nodded toward the railed enclosure at the rear.

Here Mann joined an uneasy, shuffling crowd of waiting loggers while Walter Nordyke, the firm's representative, dealt with each in turn. Nordyke was erect and tall with crow-black hair that contrasted sharply with his office-bleached complexion of dead white. His piercing black eyes seemed to read the thoughts of men grouped before the rail and paralyzed the complaining speech in their withered throats. Nick Groot, ill clad and shoulder bent, dragged forward.

"If there ain't nothing coming on my month's work I want to know the reason," he forced himself to demand. "I ain't agoing to work like this just for grub. Here I am without a damned cent and I'd like to know why."

"And I want you to know," snapped Nordyke, "that Steel and Hawley don't care a tinker's damn whether you work for them or not. If you're not suited pull out. As for your store account look here, and here, and here." The bookkeeper pointed a slender finger at an open page and read several items. "All canned stuff," he accused. "Goods that cost and don't last. Your family buys like children and you blame the firm. If you don't like your job go, and you can't go too quick." The low toned words cut like the edge of a well-honed razor.

"I didn't understand," Groot hastily justified himself. "It's the woman and youngsters. They buy everything they see. I just thought I'd ask. That's all." He stepped back and lurched away.

"Now, Mr. Winters," invited Nordyke, and a well-dressed farmer advanced and quietly handed the bookkeeper a tally sheet of logs sold by him to Steel and Hawley. When Nordyke compared it with figures in a ledger he wrote out and passed the farmer a check.

"I don't like them checks," complained Winters. "The only place nearby to get them cashed is at Bender's saloon, and Bender expects the man he accommodates to set up drinks."

"That's none of my business," said Nordyke coolly. "I don't want my throat cut some night to save you fellows from buying a drink. Currency is about as safe to handle as gunpowder in a blaze. I don't want it around."

The bookkeeper next turned to handsome, whiskey soaked Jim Sprik who leaned for support against the high rail.

"Well, Jim," he sharply accosted. "What's wanted?"

"More pay," huskily demanded Jim. "A top-loader oughta git thirty five, and I ain't paid more 'en a bush-monkey."

"Steel and Hawley don't want drunkards on the payroll," flashed Nordyke. "Understand? You'll load for what you get until you're steady. See?"

"I ain't drunk," defended Sprik indignantly. "I ain't been drunk. I'm sober as the town church. Gimme top-loader's pay or I'll bounce the job."

"Bounce and be damned," jeered the bookkeeper. "And get out!" He turned to Mann.

"Step inside," he directed, opening a gate-like half door, "and sit down. You see, Mr. Mann, I don't need an introduction. Now let's have your figures."

Mann produced his scale book and the two went over his week's work. When they finished the Blair part of the tally Mann placed beside it his recent measurement of rotten logs.

"That," he explained, "is the scale of imperfect timber Thompson sent to Blair's mill before my arrival. I knew you'd want the matter made right, so I rescaled the imperfect lot this afternoon. It was a rank deal. Either Thompson was criminally careless or a rascal."

Instead of scanning the proffered figures Nordyke turned the search-light of his penetrating gaze on the firm's new employee. After a moment's scrutiny one corner of the bookkeeper's mouth curled upward in a characteristic smile.

"You may safely leave business details to the firm," he lightly suggested. "Good evening, Mr. Mann." It was a curt dismissal.

IV

The Triple Terror of District Number Four

Saturday night in camp found the men reduced in number by those in reach of home, but enough hungry lumberjacks gathered about the long tables to keep Guy's heavy head atilt with shuffling haste. His red gums showed in his loose-mouthed grin and his pale eyes narrowed to slits between light lashes at the men's jocose demands. Hot tea, beans, cookies and primitive mince pie vanished so rapidly Long Jim eyed the diners with lively apprehension.

"I ain't figgering to fatten prize hogs," he grumbled. "Looks like they're eatin' supper and breakfast. Looks darn like they aim to swallow tomorrow's dinner too 'fore they quit."

But even a lumberjack's Saturday night appetite can be assuaged and there began the sound of tuning violins, which is like no other sound on earth. When Mann and Brinkley entered the bunk room after supper, Jet Lowney, with foot beating time, was producing soul stirring strains on a fiddle, aided by Tom Borden as second while Bud Nolan drew deep tones from a tall base viol. It was foot-tingling, inspiriting sound, and the floor instantly filled with laughing, joshing lumberjacks who formed squares and began to dance as Hod Elwin called off.

"First four right and left," he shouted from his elevated station made of boards across the water barrel. "Balance half! Ladies change across the hall," he directed amid shouts of laughter. The dancing became fast and furious. Both the "gents" and "ladies" heeled and toed in a hilarious breakdown while maddest of all was Jules Deveraux who stepped with the lightness of thistledown and the agility of a simian.

"Tance once wit me," Mann heard a voice at his elbow and turning, he saw the laughing face of the French Canadian daring him to comply. Jet Lowney struck up 'The Girl I Left Behind Me' and Mann swung into the vortex of dancers who also sang words to the old tune. Opposite him was Bob Stray. The boy's face was flushed, his eyes flashed. More insistent than ever was Mann's impression of having known the brown eyed youngster at some time in the past. The haunting resemblance troubled the scaler. If Bob received the gift of memory, what then? Was the world so small no one might find sanctuary? When Donald Brett opened the outer door and called his name Mann was glad of an excuse to leave the noisy company and, later, enjoy the quiet of his room at the manager's home.

"Well done," Brinkley hailed him as the scaler passed on the way out. "After that hoedown you may short-scale the jacks and they'll thank you. You're solid!"

Brett's handsomely matched driving team stood outside. "Thought you might as well ride over," the manager explained, "so I stopped for you." Mann thanked him and sprang into the seat at his side. As the team started in the dim light the scaler caught sight of a figure crouching in the brush, and instantly the startled horses veered from the track. Brett flashed the bull's-eye of his lantern toward the spot as the skulker hid, but not before Mann recognized the lean visage of Stimson, the rat faced swamper.

"It's Stimson," reported the scaler. "What do you suppose he expected to hear? What does he want?"

Without replying Brett swore and lashed his team to a run. When he finally addressed his companion his remarks dealt with the week's activities. Stimson was not mentioned.

Lights from the Brett log bungalow seemed ruddy hands of welcome as they neared the place, and a lusty call brought Sam blinking from his evening doze by the kitchen fire to attend the bays. As the manager had not dined he entered the kitchen for his delayed meal and Mann went to his room where he changed his lumberjack rig for civilian clothes.

"Bob isn't with you tonight," remarked Madeline when he settled in the living room with tally notes he duplicated in a book. The mistress of Log-Haven, as the bungalow was named, looked like a painting in some medieval canvas. Her gown of ruby velvet was relieved by collar and cuffs of white and both were wonderfully becoming to her vivid beauty. Mann found himself staring at this rare vision of fully blossomed womanhood until he almost forgot his mention of his pupil while Brett, having finished his meal, lapsed into the semi-torpidity of nicotine and news.

"Just now Bob's in brisk demand as a masculine belle," the scaler told his hostess, then added a graphic account of the scene in camp.

"Are you fond of music?" Madeline asked.

"Yes," Mann admitted.

"Sing some negro melodies, Madeline," demanded Brett from back of his outspread newspaper. Evening songs formed a remaining sentiment of the Brett's prosaic lives, and Madeline readily seated herself at the old piano and placed sheet music on the rack.

"Will you join me?" she asked the scaler not dreaming he would comply. But when her deep rich voice took up the air of a plantation song his cultivated bass harmonized with the swelling sound.

"Great!" Brett exclaimed at the close. "Sing another." This was for the taciturn manager extravagant praise, and his enthusiasm was shared by black Sam and his dominant wife who ecstatically beat time at the kitchen door.

Mann's singing spurred Sally to unusual endeavor in her masterly art of cooking as the scaler was invited to eat Sunday dinner with the Bretts and, later, attend the Quakeress' church service with Madeline and her servants.

Sam was to drive his master's team as the meeting was held at the district schoolhouse. And here gathered people of all sorts and beliefs by way of oxen, horses or on foot. A "meeting" was the settlers' combined opera, lecture, travelogue and club. As Madeline's team neared the log building they found the school grounds a-glimmer with converging lanterns and the still air vibrating with many voices. Men talked of logging or crops, women gossiped. Presently they sifted into the lighted room, men to the right and women to the left, on seats that reached from the center aisle to benches around the wall.

Kerosene lamps illuminated the faces of two speakers on the low platform. David Johnathan, large featured, florid, strong, and vehement in speech rose to his feet. He was the settlement circuit rider and a man of powerful influence. For a time he looked directly at his audience as if to read their thoughts. Then he gave out the lines of a stirring, martial hymn that was taken up by one and another until the low ceiling became a sounding-board of militant song. Through and above it threaded Madeline's sweet soprano supported by Mann's trained accompaniment. Settlers paused and turned in their seats to see the singers. As the last note died away, David Johnathan introduced the speaker, a Hoosier Quakeress who had journeyed into the wilderness in eager quest of converts.

The comely, compact woman in gray stepped forward and began her impassioned appeal in a voice low as wind among pines but gradually rising to a high, triumphant chant that rose and fell in musical cadence. Her flame white face and glowing eyes were transfigured. Her gray clad person was the spirit itself, and she talked of the Eternal City as if she walked its streets. Her high-pitched sing-song had an electrical effect. Many listeners were convulsively sobbing, and when she exhorted sinners to kneel at the mourner's bench a number hurried forward and sank weeping before the deal bench. Among these was Lily May, a settler's daughter, slender as the flower of her name with a wax-white countenance pure as the snow outside, baby blue eyes and unbound hair of shimmering gold. She was a beautiful devotee and appeared to need little preparation for the Hoosier's heaven.

Sharply contrasting with this moonbeam of a penitent was the vividly handsome young woman Mann discovered in the crowd and experienced a thrill of delight at her presence. The active owner of Blair's lumber mill, clad in a conventional costume of gold-brown with a twist of cardinal silk in her jaunty toque, sat demurely quiet yet her striking personality suggested verve and dash. Nothing about Blair, as she was known, was of the meek and lowly. She had been born more practical than spiritual. She was in taste and education a lumberjack, moved and had her being in logs and their product. It would be as impossible for India Blair to become a wilderness nun like Lily May as for a crimson rose to bear a violet. She nodded to the scaler as their eyes met, and smiled, but her manner was as free of coquetry as if she were but Blair of the pine-scented mill yard and he a mere business acquaintance, as he was.

At that moment attention was directed to a disturbance near the door. Three would be toughs, known in the neighborhood as The Triple Terror, began to scuffle and utter low cat calls. Rast Quick, sullen, heavy built but lame from a one-time broken limb, was the leader. Second in mischief was Bob Davitt, son of the local pugilist and a reckless dare devil, while tall, loutish Sim Parsons acted as their willing tool. Ignorant, unprincipled, craving notoriety the trio were a menace to the locality and a curse to the school. As no settler wished to antagonize the young hoodlums or their relatives they usually sinned unchallenged. Brinkley, the camp boss, however, whose inclinations were strongly religious and who invariably attended settlement meetings, strode across the room and took up an aggressive station in The Terror's midst. His frowning presence ended that evening's disorder; but both church and school were destined to suffer amazingly from The Terror's depredations.

A half hour later the rural congregation sifted slowly from the rude schoolhouse and grouped to talk of the service. Madeline Brett and India Blair exchanged hearty greetings for the two were close friends. Mann, at Mrs. Brett's side, received a friendly hand clasp from the girl lumberjack and a gay reference to their noise-enveloped meeting at the mill. Again Blair's manner was boy-like, fearless and unstudied. The scaler found himself wondering if the direct speaking girl had a woman's heart or feminine attributes. In answer to his mental query a singular incident occurred.

While the three stood in the glow of Sam's lantern chatting, Nordyke, the saturnine bookkeeper, with a nod to each, placed a possessive hand on India Blair's arm.

"Come," said he, "let me see you safely to your rig. The road is infernally dark."

Instantly Blair stepped back, dark eyes flashing and manner insolent.

"Mr. Mann has already arranged to look after me," she informed Steel and Hawley's powerful representative. "He'll untie my horse and start us off. After that Billy-boy knows the way."

The astonished tallier realized there was something significant back of the mill owner's lie and her guarded speech. But without a word of explanation regarding her conduct as they reached her rig, India helped to liberate Billy-boy, climbed in her seat and with a cool, "Good night, Mr. Mann," was off to her home at Muskrat Lake.

V

The Ginseng Diggers

Nothing is too trivial for settlement gossip. Therefore when Mrs. Slasher learned that Madeline Brett was the daughter of a physician and she herself studied books dealing with the profession the result was a call. Sally, elbow deep in suds early Monday morning, was interrupted by a knock at the door. She quickly opened it and ushered in a short fat woman wrapped in a faded shawl whose anxious, feebly smiling face was roundly framed in a once white scarf. She asked in a throaty voice for Mrs. Brett.

"Miss Lina, honey," called Sally, "har's Mis' Abe Jobbin." With this brief statement she resumed her washing as Madeline swiftly entered the room and welcomed the woman with a hearty handclasp.

"I've hern," the worried mother explained, "that you know a bit about doctoring. If you do it's God's blessing for I come to have you see my little girl. She's terrible bad off. We've tried herbs and sweating an' everything, but it's no use. She'll die if you can't save her."

Mrs. Jobbin gazed at Madeline imploringly. Her pale eyes had the pathetic look of a sheep led to slaughter.

"Being a physician's daughter don't make me a doctor," Madeline told her.

"Anyhow, you must know lots us folks never heard of," insisted the woman. "Maybe you'd think of something to do for my little Coral. She's burnt up with fever and choking to death. I left her with Em and come myself for fear you'd refuse. Do come with me, Mrs. Brett. I'll lose my baby if you don't. Do come and try." At that Mrs. Jobbin burst into wild weeping with shawl-covered face.

"I dare not assume responsibility for a life," Madeline told her.

"Then," said the mother, rising to her feet and speaking in the dull voice of utter despair, "my Coral must die. Even if we had money to pay it 'u'd be too late to git the Hickory Vale doctor. I hern you lost a little one. I hoped you'd – that anyway you'd try."

The last remark won her cause. The reference to Madeline's lost babe decided her. "I'll at least go home with you," she declared. "I'll have a look at the child. That won't do any harm if it don't help." She quickly donned overshoes and wraps while Mrs. Jobbin expressed voluble gratitude but Sally regarded the arrangement with apprehension.

"Laws now, Miss Liney, you orter hab de hosses," she objected. "W'y don' you wait twell Marse Brett gits home an' tek you ober?"

"I can't delay," said Madeline. "Minutes are precious."

This was doubly true. She could not wait for her husband's arrival as he would forbid her mission. She must act, if at all, at once or never. Over two miles of snow the two women hastened until they reached a square built log cabin in a small clearing. A shepherd dog fawned on them at the bars and two hogs scuttled from their path. Within the rude cabin a passive, bovine face was turned to greet them.

"Coral's most gone," the neighbor, Mrs. May, told them in sick room whispers. "I come over to help but guess nothing'll do good. The poor babe can't fight for breath no more." Mrs. May, who was mother of the slender devotee at the schoolhouse revival, stood with arms akimbo and looked on while Madeline examined the strangling infant.

"Bring hot water, dry mustard and a tub," Madeline requested. Fear of her incompetence vanished. She roused to the situation. With steady hands she removed the babe's clothing and placed the clammy infant in the warm bath. The women stared agape. Only supreme faith in Madeline's supposed knowledge induced Mrs. Jobbin to permit such drastic measures. Water was little esteemed in most settlement homes. Bodily application was a long deferred rite, and in time of illness both water and fresh air were carefully avoided.

Em Jobbin, gaunt, tall and shyly awkward, produced such articles as Mrs. Brett from time to time demanded while Dan bashfully tiptoed out for wood, and on a stool by the stove sat a demure midget barely graduated from the cradle. Her chubby arms were crossed on her small chest and her button-black eyes eagerly observed the curious scene. At last the battle waged with water, friction and a woolen blanket gave

Madeline the victory. Coral opened her pain-wracked blue eyes and lifted feeble hands toward her mother to be taken.

"That's sure a miracle," Mrs. Jobbin gratefully declared. "It beats all I ever seen. Why, that baby ain't moved before since midnight!"

With the tenderness of one who has snatched a life back from the beyond, Madeline pressed the infant to her breast. It had become her own – born of her agonized endeavor. From that hour she determined to make use of her inherited gift.

"Your babe is safe," she told the relieved mother. "Keep her warm. Give her water to drink when she asks for it. I'll see her tomorrow if possible."

Madeline's "if" was a fortunate reservation. Donald Brett, driving home, overtook his wife, helped her to a seat by his side in the low cutter, then with darkening brow heard the story of her ministrations. The words came falteringly because she sensed his black anger at her disobedience to his wishes. His silence was a mask of ice. He hated female publicity, especially for Madeline.

"Let this end such nonsense," he said briskly and coldly. "I don't want you to become that travesty – a quack doctor."

"But the Jobbins' would have lost their child," she pleaded. "The babe was dying."

An ironical expression overspread Brett's masterful countenance – a look of disdainful incredulity. Seeing his unbelief Madeline ceased trying to make him understand her motives. Upon reaching home she removed her wraps and flung herself on the broad couch to rest and indulge in loving thoughts of the tiny creature she had restored to pulsing life. If not her actions she might at least control her mental processes for, deep in the core of her intellect, she harbored dreams and aspirations which Brett never suspected. So the eternal brain wheel revolved in secret rather than offend. Natural combativeness in her strong nature impelled her to independent thought and the working out of her own ideas, but she was too fine for open aggression. Now, as she reviewed the day's happenings visions came to her of the pretty garments she would make for the child reborn, her half-adopted babe and the old fashioned midget who sat with folded arms by the stove.

In a short time she got up and went about the dainty task of table setting. Under shaded lights she placed gilt edged dishes with the Brett monogram, then a square of golden honey in cut glass, flanked by crimson jelly and feather-light gingerbread. To this Sally added a plate of her wonderful waffles and a rich brown fricassee accompanied by mashed potatoes banked like snow. To the end of time Madeline remembered every item of that evening meal even to the aromatic coffee, praised by Brett, and its addition of yellow cream. She was fated to be glad of its excellence and that she repressed her resentment and was frankly gay. They were barely through dinner and settled in the living room when Mann and his pupil, Bob Stray, arrived from camp.

"The weather's an arctic blizzard since dark," the scaler reported. "Winter's trying to get rooted in December."

"It's too early," The manager responded in his peculiar manner of unexpectedly joining a conversation from behind his newspaper. "Genuine winter comes on wet ground and this one fell on frost.

Snow on frozen turf goes, on water soaked ground it stays."

Bob and his teacher retired to the scaler's room where a dull mumble back of the closed door told of a reading lesson in progress. Bob learned readily. He absorbed facts as if he merely renewed what he had at some time mastered. Other studies occupied an hour, after which teacher and pupil emerged from retirement and Brett demanded singing.

"Not that classical stuff," he objected, noting his wife's selection. "Sing something with a heart in it. Sing 'Robin Adair.'"

Amazed, Madeline searched among her music for the ancient song. Never before had Donald asked for the gloomy lines. But she found it and immediately the sweet, pessimistic words vibrated in the raftered room as she and Forrest Mann sang in perfect accord. Afterward Madeline was to recall her husband's strange choice and with travail of soul wonder if to him the words of 'Robin Adair' were significant, and if he meant them to hold meaning for her, his wife.

"What's this dull town to me, Robin's not near?" the voices sang in exquisite harmony. "Where's all the joy and mirth that made this place a heaven on earth? Oh, they're all fled with thee, Robin Adair."

"Have you a favorite you'd like to have us try out?" Madeline asked the tallyman when the last note of 'Robin Adair' trembled into space.

"Thank you, I believe not," Mann answered. "I'm trying to forget both home and its songs."

That moment Mrs. Brett had the sensation of one who blunders into a secret room. She felt inexcusably tactless. To cover her confusion she struck the chords of a famous plantation song. Instantly the kitchen door swung wide revealing Sam in his arm chair beating time with his bald head and black hands.

"Dat ol' black Joe, dat's me," he declared imaginatively at the close. "Lots o' times I c'n har dem voices in the de night."

"Shucks," his wife jeered. "Yo' don' har no sich noises. Hit's mo' 'en I c'n do to wuck yo' up mornings by hollerin'."

Bob Stray waited until the singing ended, then started back through the snow flurry to camp. It was what woodsmen call a wet snow that acted on former snows like melting rain. Everywhere the white covering had settled until Bob's lantern showed dark hillocks in the woods. He wondered at the evening's blizzard so quickly turning to a thaw, then fell to speculating where he had before heard Forrest Mann's incomparable singing but the memory was exasperatingly elusive. For the thousandth, or ten thousandth, time he reviewed the two years of his known past. First he found himself in a rough lumbering camp farther down in the state. Later he drifted north with workmen until he obtained employment with Steel and Hawley where he remained and studied his unsolvable problem. This night it obtruded itself persistently as he hastened along the rutted road. Presently his swinging foot came in contact with a clod of packed snow and earth that had formed on some horse's shod hoof. Instantly, by impulse, he kicked the oval clod until it rose and fell far away with a dull thud. His booted toe stung from the impact. Astonished at his involuntary performance he stood stock still.

"Now why," he asked himself, "did I do that insane act?"

He had been impelled by subconscious influence. Some time in his life he had been familiar with that particular movement. Puzzled, resentful at his inability to apply the clue, he walked swiftly on to camp, retired to his bunk, and soon slept from sheer weariness.

Sunday dawned in a burst of sunshine that counterfeited spring. Patches of bare ground crowded the remaining snow into hollows and Indian summer warmth converted spoiled roads into rivulets. Knowing it was the last genial spell before grim winter, Mann determined to strike in back of camp and enjoy a tramp in the woods. As he passed by the bunk house on his way from Brett's where he had breakfasted, several lumberjacks had swung kettles over outdoor fires and were engaged at their week's wash. Mike Munshaw, with sleeves rolled up and his head in a steam cloud, pounded and vigorously rubbed his weekday flannel then soused it from the suds and plumped it into a violently boiling kettle.

"Say, you ignorant galoot," yelled Long Jim from his cook house, "you'll spile that shirt! Don't you know biling ain't good for wool?"

"Neither 'tain't good for varmints," argued Mike. "It frets 'em fierce," said he, and began on the next garment.

Leaving Mike to his discussion of entomology Mann crossed the slash and climbed a hill into the pine-scented forest. The exertion set his blood tingling and his lungs pumping air like old wine. As he paused a glimpse of Muskrat Lake gave him a definite purpose. He would explore the Blair holdings to be lumbered by Steel and Hawley. Blazed trees would mark the boundary if he could find them. Under his feet was a thick russet carpet of sweet smelling leaves patched with snow. About him were gray bodied giants soon to be felled by a crew of lumberjacks for the rival mills. Everywhere bird calls, chattering squirrels and crackling brush emphasized the strange hush of a great forest. On and on he tramped until aching bones suggested something was amiss. Reluctantly he admitted to himself that he was lost and roundly cursed his stupidity. He turned and tried to track himself homeward. Impossible! The leaf carpet left no trail and he had avoided snow. Disgusted, he moved forward while a squirrel burst into a frenzy of chatter and a sudden flash of red told him a deer had sped by to new feeding grounds.

"Probably joining a herd inland," thought the scaler, and turned in an opposite direction.

He recalled a woodcraft saying that tips of hemlocks bent away from the prevailing winds and that moss grew on the north side of tree trunks; but the hemlocks he examined pierced the sky with ramrod precision and moss for once failed to protect the trees. The forenoon's burst of sunshine had long before disappeared and the thick timber grayed to twilight as the scaler stumbled on, hungry and desperately tired. He decided that he must be traveling in a circle as he had heard of strayed men doing when he came upon freshly turned leaves.

"Shang hunters," he thought and was encouraged. He followed the root digger's trail until he sighted two bend forms busied at extracting wild ginseng from its native turf. The faces that lifted at his call were swarthy with outdoor living and exceedingly repellent. Afterward he learned the two were Turner and Wells, leaders of the Turn-Well cattle thieves and famous shangers who haunted the forest.

"I'm lost," Mann briefly explained.

"Then you must be a damn greenhorn," one of the men told him in evident disgust, standing upright, long boned and wiry. He stared at Mann with suspicious, unblinking eyes.

The other shanger also rose stiffly and scrutinized the interloper with open enmity. "Who in hell are you?" he demanded.

"I'm Steel and Hawley's scaler," he told them.

At this the outlaws eyed him with interest.

"Maybe you be," admitted the land shanger, "but I'll swear you ain't Nordyke's picking."

"If you'll kindly direct me," Mann hinted.

"Muskrat Lake's a mile off that way," pointed the root digger. "And when you're out of the woods forget you saw us. We ain't hunting shang beds for other fellers to profit on; so we don't want no damn prowlers. See?"

Mann nodded. He knew shang patches were jealously guarded and hard to find. In return for the shangers' aid he emptied his pockets of coin and handed the sum to the nearest cattle rustler, the shorter and heavier of the two.

"Guess we better show him out," suggested the lank digger. "You go ahead and I'll carry the roots."

Thus escorted Mann was marched in a puzzling detour until a thinning wall of timber showed the light of a clearing. Glad to escape a night in the woods he took leave of the outlaws and hastened through the sparse grove. Midway he became aware of low pitched voices and soon discovered two men in earnest conversation. Even in the dim light he easily recognized Stimson, the skulking bush-monkey, and Nordyke, the firm's bookkeeper. As they perceived his proximity Stimson's ferret face paled to the tint of unbaked dough but Nordyke, insolent and nonchalant, confronted the intruder.

"Fine day for a hike in the woods," he remarked derisively.

"Yes," said Mann, and attempted to pass.

"Indulged in a walk myself," volunteered Nordyke. "I sent for a guide and examined a mile or so of timber the firm thinks of buying." He persisted in making the needless statement, then stepped aside and permitted the scaler to proceed.

But Mann, hurrying toward camp and his belated supper, knew the bookkeeper lied. His plausible account failed to convince. Mystified at Nordyke's evasion, he reached camp and ate so voraciously Long Jim observed his appetite with amazement.

"Act like you're stowing grub for a cruise," he commented. "Never saw your beat but once and he was a starved Injun."

"Going to meeting?" asked Brinkley when Mann re-entered the bunk room. Instantly the scaler remembered the girl lumberjack. He might see her, so he forgot this tired muscles and the two set forth.

They were late. The big circuit rider whose florid face was foreshortened by the kerosene table lamp, shouted out a series of climatic periods while his strong hands flailed the desk or violently gesticulated. In the midst of his impassioned oratory the Three Terrors began their pranks. Rast Quick, the lame lad, evolved jokes which his two aids executed. His last was in the form of a drawing he had made of David Johnathan. It was a fair likeness. Bob Davitt was slyly pinning this caricature of the energetic divine to the rear wall when the high-pitched tones of the speaker suddenly ceased. With a dash he left the platform, grasped Quick and Davitt by their collars and rapped their astonished heads together with resounding whacks. He then resumed his discourse at the point of interruption, but the aching head of Rast Quick demanded vengeance which he would ultimately put into effect.

The startled audience gasped at the strange interlude, and Percy Tinkham, the pale teacher from Hickory Vale who weekly suffered from the evil doings of the Three Terrors, witnessed the scene with joy. The sound of those crashing heads vastly relieved his tortured spirit. But to Forrest Mann the evening was a disappointment. The vivid face, the dark eyes, the friendly hands in gauntlets were missing. India Blair was not present.

VI

Spiked Logs at Blair's Mill

During early winter sickness in the settlement was epidemic and Madeline freely, if secretly, responded to the more urgent calls for help. At that date no medical diploma was required of self-taught physicians so she was at liberty to act. Except for Donald. She knew he was aware of her disobedience to his wishes but he made no sign. One morning at breakfast, however, Sally admitted Lem Hixon, intent upon securing the woman doctor's assistance for an only son. Nervously he fumbled his cloth cap as he stood just within the door and haltingly made known his errand.

"My wife is not a medical practitioner," Brett coldly asserted. "She cannot go."

"The boy's mighty bad," urged Hixon. "An' he's the only ---. His mother'll never quit grieving if ---."

"Send for Armstrong," cut in Brett. He named the Hickory Vale physician. "If you haven't a team, I'll see that there is one supplied. But my wife can't act."

Sadly the woodsman turned and passed out. His despair wrung Madeline's heart. Impulse inclined her to spring up and go to the lad's bedside. She glanced at her husband and marveled at the expression of suppressed wrath in his stern countenance. Instinctively she quailed before the lowering storm. For days they had been out of step. She fancied they antagonized each other more than usual. A burst of accusing words from him would have been a relief, would have cleared the air. But under this cold, unspoken anger she was helpless. It excited her to rebellion. After Brett departed, she dressed in heavy attire, put on rubber footwear and started lakeward in the direction of the Hixon's cabin. Bill Watson, the curly haired teamster, overtook her and gave her a ride on his load of logs to a cross track leading northward, and finally she reached her destination. The battered door was opened at her knock by Mrs. Hixon. She was extraordinarily lean with prominent bones and a rag covering, while her "hank o' hair" was twisted in a tight knob at the back of her head.

"I've come to see Tommy," announced the manager's wife.

"Then the Almighty ain't quite forsook us," said the woman and began to weep. For hours Madeline, assisted by the mother and a neighbor, worked hopelessly for the boy's life. Hixon had gone for the doctor and was evidently delayed. Finally Dr. Armstrong arrived with his medicine case and administered stimulants that had an immediate effect. His big, clean shaven face was placid with assured success. His presence radiated courage. His powerful bulk seemed to dwarf the room.

"Two hours ago the lad was dying," he told Madeline, "but you held him. You kept him from slipping over the brink. Now your work is finished. Go home and rest." He smiled and his calm gaze accepted Madeline as a co-worker. She felt repaid.

Lem Hixon, jubilant and grateful at his son's safety, took her home with the borrowed team. On the way they passed Brett. His averted face was black with wrath. He was deaf to the glad report his wife called to him of the sick boy as he slipped by and dashed onward toward Agache.

To Madeline's relief her husband utterly ignored the Hixon affair. She hoped her success in saving a life excused her from further blame. If she had failed to hold Tommy Hixon from death his blood would be on her hands as surely as if she killed him. Brett's silence was like a reprieve; but he was fully occupied with Steel and Hawley business – and worried.

Enough snow fell that week to rouse camp activities. Extra teams hauled logs to the lake and to Blair's mill. Mann and Bob Stray scaled and stamped skidways from morning to night, and Brett kept ceaselessly on the move watching every part of the work. Being much alone, Madeline became absorbed in the pages of her favorite science. She forgot time and place, and one evening Brett found her before the book covered table but refrained from comment. His strong countenance was, however, eloquent of his morbid hatred for his wife's obsession. She swept the books from sight while in the kitchen Aunt Sally scolded her long-suffering husband and his deeper tones evaded, pleaded and blustered.

"Hussle in dat wood 'fore hit sprouts lak de staff o' Moses," ordered Sam's dusky wife. She jerked a lid from the cook stove and peered at the diminishing fire, then prodded the contents of simmering kettles.

"Ain't no call ter hussle," complained Sam. "I jes tuk in mo' wood 'en yo' need the nex hour. Dat dar box am half full."

"Anyhow, hit's time yo' git a pail o' water; an' min' yo' don' slop none on dis yer clean flo'."

"Wish to goodness you'd stop scrubbin'," mourned Sam. "Hit uses up a sight mo water 'en dere's any sense in. Sides dere ain' no way fo' me to git 'roun dis flo' lessen I stomp on hit. I ain't no bird."

"No," heartily agreed his wife, "yo' ain't no bird, dat's shuah. Mos' any pusson could tell dat by lookin' at yo'." Sally's fat sides shook with laughter. Sam, featured as a winged biped, upset her gravity. So as humor and ill temper, like solids, can't occupy the same space peace descended on the Brett Kitchen.

When the scaler arrived with his tally sheets, Madeline sat before the living room grate with slippered feet on the guard. Her gown of cream colored silk and black lace gave her round throat the hue of a white rose leaf. Her slender fingers held material of which she was making a dainty dress for little Coral. It was delightful employment and her dark eyes were softly meditative.

"You see I'm early," said Mann with an admiring glance at his hostess. "I finished the Blair rollway and thought I'd jot them down in my books." He began transferring notes at the baize-covered table and the Blair account incited him to praise one woman to another.

"India Blair is a wonderful girl," he commented.

"And she's the daughter of a brave man," Madeline responded. Dropping her work in her lap she told the scaler of Blair's rise from workman to mill owner, of his mortgaging his mill and two sections of land in order to install modern machinery. Steel and Hawley were to pay themselves in timber and also to deliver logs to Blair's mill. These logs were to be paid for in the Blair cut of lumber; but after the bargain was down in black and white Blair was murdered.

"Murdered!" echoed Mann.

"Yes; to all intents and purposes Blair was murdered."

"Why the uncertainty?" questioned Mann.

"Because," said Madeline, "he was killed by his steel saw bursting on an imbedded spike. His enemy – whoever that might be – drove iron in the logs knowing Blair was his own sawyer, and he was killed by flying steel. Before breath left his body he told India to continue the business. She was his idol, his duplicate in appearance, courage and disposition. He had given her the advantage of Manistee schools so she kept his books. No one marveled at India going on with the mill. It was the only way to keep a home and pay the debts."

"Miss Blair is a wonder," repeated the scaler. He recalled the vision of India in her lumber yard costume, her lithe movements, the spirited glint of her dark eyes, her decisive, imperious gestures. He remembered her ruse at the schoolhouse door to rid herself of Nordyke. Her daring impertinence thrilled him. Surely such a girl could outwit her enemies.

"I dare not permit myself the luxury of the girl lumberjack's friendship," mused the tally-man, "but if I can step between her and evil – who's other name seems Nordyke – I am at her service."

For hours Brett busied himself with bundles of papers in his desk then asked his wife to sing, to sing especially 'Robin Adair'.

"That Robin song is heart-breaking," complained Madeline. "I can't bear it."

"Hearts don't break," Brett commented dryly. "A healthy mind readjusts itself. Only fools go mad."

After the song was ended he looked up from his papers to ask Mann a question.

"What's the total scale of those fraudulent rollways at Blair's mill?" he demanded, eyes fixed of the scaler.

"Eighty five thousand," Mann told him.

"Did Nordyke accept your deduction?"

"He told me to let the figures talk and mind my own affairs."

Brett swore. He turned about and again addressed himself to documents in his desk.

"There's no love lost between Brett and Nordyke," decided Mann. "Neither does he favor India Blair. Why?" He mulled the problem until sleep stopped the machinery of thought. Then in the snapping cold of morning he resumed the puzzle among new skidways.

"That skid's ready for the 'S.H.'," he called to Bob Stray, "and when it's stamped I'll have one waiting for the 'B.'"

It was a rush hour. Empty bunks were returning for logs and heavy chained loads were passing out to the lake. Everywhere was heard the high pitched, musical chime of cross-cut saws and the booming crash of falling timber. But there was no response from Bob Stray because he had joined an excited group whose core was Watson and his team.

"Balsam's sawed into another spike," passed from mouth to mouth. Then Hilliker's loud voice demanded, "Who's killed?"

"Nobody," Watson's thin treble gave back. "But Balsam had to go to Hickory Vale and have Doc Armstrong sew him up besides digging pieces of that sixty dollar saw outen his arms."

"Beat's hell," exploded Ben Heald. "I'd swear there ain't a sneak in the hull settlement mean enough to spike the Blair logs."

"Mony a mon likes to earn a bit extra," McManus quietly asserted. "There's plenty to be hired for foul work."

"Just what do you mean?" asked the scaler who had drawn near.

"I'm no talkin' for pooblication," the big Scotchman reminded him. "But there's no mon in camp but kens the deed was hired."

"Who's his employer?" Mann asked a pertinent query, but a dead silence followed. Not a lumberjack present was willing to voice an accusation. They were not mentioning names.

"What's the penalty for log-spiking?" was Mann's next question.

"State's prison," several promptly responded. Evidently they were familiar with the subject.

"It's a penitentiary job," Dan Hilliker told him.

Long Jim's dinner horn scattered the gathering, but not until Mann observed that Stimson, the swamper, was silently devouring every word concerning the near tragedy. His attitude was that of an eavesdropper who listened with eyes as well as ears seeking the undertow of public opinion. The evil, listening face had the effect of sending the tally-man down the valley road to the Blair mill with its swarm of excited workers, its screech of exhausting steam, the roar of a saw rending the heart of a pine. The noisy activity astonished him. If Balsam was wounded surely there was no one to fill his dangerous station even if a new saw replaced the one shattered by a spike. Wonderingly he ascended to the working floor and looked toward the slashing saw. Then he stared in blank amazement. India Blair, herself, in her short-skirted corduroy and high laced boots stood at the lever!

The girl's handsome face was set and angry as her dark eyes watched the advancing log and her firm hand guided the screaming circle of steel through the length of timber. A second and third board joined the slow moving river of yellow lumber that flowed down a slide before she glanced up and perceived the scaler. Instantly she signaled to Matt Crane, the setter, to take her place while an Indian stepped on the log-carriage.

"I've been hoping you'd come," India told Mann when she reached his side. "We'll go where we can talk without shouting," said she and started for the stair, motioning him to follow. When at last she paused at the river side he saw that she was pale with anxiety and her dark eyes heavy.

"You're a friend in time of need," she said gravely. "No one else can advise me or help because they are too near the trouble, and too prejudiced for cool judgement."

"I came to help," said Mann.

"I knew you would," said India. "You see my men are powerless. They're helpless to defend themselves or me. The enemy that is stalking my mother and myself to ruin would strike them down because they are in the way. That rollway scale was no error. These spiked logs are part of a scheme to frighten us into relinquishing our holdings. Steel and Hawley intend to wipe out a rival and gain a coveted tract of timber."

"Is it possible they would connive at criminal methods?" asked the amazed scaler.

"That's what I want you to prove," cried India. "Help me to find the man who spikes the timber. I'm sure the crime is accomplished before the logs leave the woods. When the log-spiker is identified we'll know his master."

"Of course Brett is ignorant of this delivery," said Mann.

"Donald Brett disapproves of me heartily," asserted India.

The scaler understood. Steel and Hawley's manager hated business women, therefore he would hate India. "But," insisted Mann, "Brett's above suspicion. He'd never countenance foul play."

India's next words astonished him. "I can't quite trust even Madeline's husband. That's why I appeal to you, a stranger, instead of going to the manager. He may be above foul play but I can't confide in him."

"If day and night vigilance counts I'll spot the criminal," promised the scaler.

"But I'm afraid for you," cried India. "The guilty tool will be a desperate, dangerous outlaw. I'm mad to ask you such a favor. But," with a hopeless gesture, "there is no one else – not one."

In that moment Mann's deep blue eyes flooded with something more than compassion. "Your confidence honors me," he told her. "And my being a stranger is in our favor. No one will suspect my interest or observe my watching. But if I am to discover the man responsible for your father's death, you must avoid danger, protect his daughter."

"He's that – my father's murderer," she admitted with a quick glance at the speaker. "And because they murder I'll win. Spiked logs shan't stop the cut of timber that's to save the mill. I'll see to that."

"No," Mann commanded. "You're not to risk your life. If I act for you I must know you are safe. Promise."

"Balsam and Matt Crane are the only ones who will stand back of iron filled timber," she told him. "My life's of no more value than theirs. I'll show them that I won't put them in danger and play safe. Don't ask it."

"I demand it," cried the scaler. He caught the gauntlet covered hand in a stinging clasp, then left the girl lumberjack by the sluggish river and retraced his way to camp. He dared not meet her gaze because his eyes were love-filled and his strong arms ached to hold and shield her. Better far that his sentiment had been hate. Again he determined to suppress his growing passion at all cost. Who was he that he permitted love in his heart for India Blair?

That evening Brinkley caught up with Mann as he threaded the slash and walked in the deepening twilight as his side.

"Sky's full of snow," remarked the boss. He gazed upward at piling cumuli. "All day them little gray puffballs of snow birds was thicker 'en skeeters. I reckoned something was up and likely to come down. 'Bout time, too."

"My man isn't Brinkley," thought the scaler. "He'd harm neither Indian Blair or a snow bird."

At that moment a stooping form slouched by with the slinking tread of a lynx. He squeaked a falsetto greeting to the two men as if anxious to appear friendly.

"Neither is my log-spiker Stimson," decided Mann, watching the bush-monkey's scurrying form. "He's a fool while the spiker is adroit, keen witted, subtle and daring. Who is he?"

VII

Where is Donald Brett?

That same week two more exciting events electrified the neighborhood. First of these was the bursting of another saw in the Blair mill. Balsam, this time, escaped the flying steel but Matt Crane came within an inch of death. Examination of the timber showed that an ordinary file had been driven in the log from shaft to tip. The sight of it infuriated Sam Crisp, the Blair filer.

"The dod-binged, blasted galoot," he bellowed. "If the dum-guzzled son-of-a-gun is hinting that I can't file saws he's a liar."

"Hold your tongue," snapped Balsam, "and rush another saw. Them logs is going to turn into boards if they're full of spikes as a porcupine has quills. I'd saw cast iron if someone had the nerve to ride the carriage."

At the word Shawnoga, the swarthy half breed, stepped to Matt Crane's place and lifted the cant-hook ready for a log. Thus Mann, on his arrival at the scene of the near tragedy, found the mill going full blast with every man but Crane at his post. Balsam, stern of face with deep set eyes and the manner of one deafened by years are his present task, slowly levered the dangerous timbers toward the third new saw. His right arm was still bandaged but his nervous hand firmly grasped the lever bar. Nearby, anxiously watching the turn of events, stood India Blair. Her vivid face was pale and beneath the dark eyes were half circles like bruised flesh. Seeing Mann she joined him and the two descended the mill stairway and walked beyond the mill's insistent roar.

"You see I failed," Mann said despondently.

"It might have been worse," she reminded him. "It shows what to expect."

"Perhaps after all there's treachery in your own mill yard." suggested the scaler.

"Are you certain the log was freshly cut?"

"It was from Jim Sprik's last load. Come," she gestured, "I'll show you the tampered log. The log and file may furnish some clue."

At the foot of the lumber slide a pine lay with the deadly steel exposed. To Mann's amazement he recognized the slightly curved timber as one he scaled the day before. He was sure of it.

"That file is like dozens of such tools owned by workmen. Identifying it would be like hunting a special leaf in the forest. My only way is to catch the scoundrel red-handed by keeping watch at night," decided the out-witted scaler.

"You can't work days and stand guard nights," cried India.

"The spiker will not act during a soft snow like the one that fell last night," explained Mann. "He won't risk pounding iron into green wood on a frosty night. Besides, he'll work between midnight and four o'clock. I'll sleep till twelve."

"Be careful," implored India. "The log-spiker would kill you to shield himself. There must be some other way. I can't have you murdered while defending my property."

"I won't be," smiled the scaler. "I shall take excellent care that I'm not discovered." He spoke lightly to relieve the girl's not altogether groundless anxiety. A few seconds later India stood looking at the gloved hand Mann had crushed I his warm palm. Her red lips curved in an oddly contented smile considering her accumulating troubles, and she suddenly lifted the leather glove to her burning face.

When Forrest Mann entered the Brett cottage at the usual hour he found himself confronting another mystery.

"Why do you suppose Donald is late?" Madeline questioned him. Her voice had the sharp note of intense anxiety.

"He should be home," said the scaler, "for he hasn't been near camp since noon."

"He was here to lunch," explained the manager's wife. "Right afterward he went away on foot leaving his team in the barn." She lifted worried eyes to the tallier's face. "He always drives. Why did he go without the horses?"

"Possibly he rode into Agache with a camp team," suggested Mann. "Let me take the bays and see if he's at the company's store. When we know his movements you'll find that you worried needlessly. Everything will be all right."

Madeline felt reassured. Her anxiety was partly moody dread induced by the happenings at Blair's mill. Donald had often remained away late, but always with his team. That was the strange, unexplained part of the situation. When she heard Mann drive toward Agache she crushed back a haunting premonition of evil and settled on the couch to await her husband's homecoming.

But the night passed, the following anxious day wore on to noon yet nothing was learned of the manager's movements. By that time Madeline was half crazed by fear for her husband's safety. He must be ill, perhaps on some lonely trail. Only Mann's objection restrained her from taking up the search in person. At camp the men worked and audibly wondered.

"Brett gave me enough directions about the work to last a week," Brinkley told the scaler. He glanced at Mann with a look of sharp significance. "That's a fact. He went through the woods planning this and that. Darned queer. Looked to me like he aimed to take a trip."

"Then why didn't you say so?" cried Mann angrily. "Anyway how could he leave the settlement without his team or a hired rig?"

"The whole affair looks blamed peculiar," burst out Brinkley. "First spiked logs from our skids near kills two men, then the manager skips out. So far as the team is concerned a man like Brett could easily walk to the station or hire a ride. If he did we'll hear from it. But there's forty ways Brett could get off and no one be the wiser. I don't like the look of it."

That afternoon Madeline Brett wrote several telegrams of inquiry and Mann again drove to Agache to have them dispatched. At the company's story he handed them to Nordyke for transmission. The bookkeeper, who was likewise telegraph operator, clicked off the words but his thin lips lifted at the corner in a sardonic smile. After the disheartening answers came back, one by one, and were written on correct forms Nordyke dispatched a message of his own composition, addressed to Mark Steel, the senior partner of the firm. Could Mann have interpreted the Morse code his final query might have been partly answered.

"Do you know where Brett is?" he abruptly demanded of the bookkeeper.

"No," flared Nordyke. "I'm not Brett's keeper!"

In the big store where Ridman waited on customers with is usual rapidity, Mann paused to gather up several purchases.

"Mighty queer about Brett," Ridman remarked. "Get him on the wire?"

Mann shook his head. As the store was filled with farmers, lumbermen and Indians he was not inclined to discuss the manager's disappearance. So he passed on without speech, but when he reached the door Ridman was at this side.

"Keep this to yourself," he told the scaler in low quick utterance. "But I know Nordyke's glad Brett skipped. He hopes he'll never come back. They didn't hitch worth a cent. I've heard them jangling in the office many a time with the door shut. Them two hate each other like poison. That's my opinion if it's any good."

Ridman's opinion, at least, gave Mann material for worried thought. If Brett and Nordyke failed to agree about the firm's business the former might have quit his position in swift disgust. But as the idea came it perished. Brett was not a fugitive, he was a fighter. On the heels of this crept the sinister thought that scores of men deliberately vanish every year. They drop from sight like pebbles in mid-ocean and their motives are legion. Some wish to begin unhampered lives, they fly from business embarrassments, they sever domestic relations that have become intolerable. Which of these incentives urged Brett to the mad deed? Surely not the last--.

At this point the scaler's imagination failed him. Each theory he evolved was more insultingly inconsistent than the other. He concluded no one might guess correctly why Brett dropped from sight. He doubtless would in time clear his motives to everyone's satisfaction.

When the days sped by with no wired or written communication from her taciturn husband Madeline's heart-wrenching suspicion changed to certainty. She believed herself deserted beyond a shadow of doubt. Through nightmare days and nights she ceaselessly revolved the hideous, unspoken thought. Bit by bit she recalled Donald's separate, absorbed existence, his bitter dislike of her pastimes, ambitions, studies and sentiment. His hatred for her amateur medical practice loomed black on her mental horizon. Hour by hour she tried to see wherein she had been false to her marriage vow. She placed herself before a pitiless bar of justice and was devoutly thankful that her conscience acquitted her of intentional wrong doing.

After a time the thought that she had been cast off by the man who had sworn to love and protect her roused her southern pride. Indignation helped her to partly rally from the shock of Brett's desertion. If he desired to be free she would try not to eat her heart out by useless repining. So she gained strength to face financial considerations. Sam and Sally were dependent on her fortunes. She must face the future for their sakes if not her own. Therefore Mann, at her request, assisted her to examine the manager's papers. They were in perfect order and concerned the affairs of Steel and Hawley. Diligent search revealed nothing more. Although Brett had received a generous salary they found no records of bank deposits or investments. Finally they were forced to the conclusion that he had taken his savings with him. His wife owned the farm home, the team and her husband's salary for the unpaid quarter. That was all.

"You'll sell out and return South -- to your former home," suggested Mann.

"No," cried Madeline. "I shall stay here among people who knew him. If he wants me he'll find me in my home. My parents are dead and my friends must never know – this shame. I'll find employment. Sam can raise a garden and we'll stay on the farm."

Mann regarded the woman across the paper-littered table with profound respect. The ivory pallor of her delicate face alone betrayed her spiritual crucifixion. The handsome head was proudly poised, and smoldering fire burned in the black eyes.

"No soldier under arms ever possessed higher courage," he praised. "May God help you."

What she had said to Mann was the nearest approach Madeline made to voicing her convictions. Others might think what they pleased but the stricken wife sealed the hideous truth within her breast. To Sally and India Blair her white face was eloquent of suffering and testified to her belief, but no word passed of the horror that preyed on her tortured mind.

Sally disposed of the matter in her own original way. With the diplomacy of a diplomat she retained well-meaning news seekers in the background of her kitchen where she supplied them with information of reckless manufacture.

"No'm," she informed Mrs. Swisher. "Miss Liney ain't sick an' she ain' going ter be sick. She jus' got 'er bilious fit. I tol' 'er to stay kivvered up an' stop talking. I's allus tended 'er bilious fits ebber since she were born, an' there ain' no call to worry. She'll git ober it right smart."

Having relieved her own mind – and the caller's – she applied a scrubbing brush to the cook table with vicious energy. In the midst of her onslaught a second knock sounded, and this time Mrs. May, ponderous and asthmatic, entered the room with a rolling gait and subsided in the chair Sally offered. The two neighbors began to exchange neighborhood items of common interest.

"There's going to be a big time at the New Year's dance in Agache." Mrs. Swisher made known. "Everybody far and near's a going. Settlement folks 'u'd dance if they were dying. What they'd do in Kingdom Come without a dance hall is more 'en I know. I reckon they'll ask the angel band to play 'Money Musk' or 'The Devil's Reel' and they'll start frisking round before St. Peter gathers his wits to stop them."

"Folks has to have some enjoyment," defended Mrs. May, creaking back and forth in her rocker. "My Lil's going, but she ain't allowed to have a beau – not at her age. She's going with her brothers. When a girl has seven grown up brothers to take care o' her she's well off."

"I wouldn't wonder," observed Mrs. Swisher, "if India Blair 'u'd go to the dance with Walt Nordyke. He's crazy about her and I don't think she'd refuse him."

"India Blair would dare anything," declared Mrs. May. "She ain't no coward, not much. And to my mind she's kind o' brazen."

"Expect Mr. Brett home soon?" she directed toward Sally, thus approaching the real object of her visit.

"No'm," Sally stated with decision. "Marse Brett ain' comin' back fo' a right smart spell. Yes'm, course we know where he hatter go. Finanshul difficulty bodder mo' folks 'en yo' know 'bout. Dat's de truf. Lak de Bible says money's de root ob ebil, an' pears to branch out scandalous."

The visitors were not deceived. When the Brett door closed behind them and they were on their way they talked of the strange affair in low tones with head shakes. In half sentences they pointed to the cause for the manager's absence that Mann completely overlooked.

"I donno's as I blame him for being jealous," murmured Mrs. May. "Brett wasn't no beauty, an' the new scaler's handsome as they make 'em and mighty pleasant. No' I dunno as I blame him for getting off the earth, and I dunno's I blame her for liking Mann best. Brett was a grouch – short and sharp."

"Fiddlesticks," scoffed Mrs. Swisher. "You'd smell a rat in a rosebush, stead of flowers. Like everyone else I think Brett's skipped, but you take my word it ain't because he's making a present of his wife to another man; not he."

When Sally was alone she thrust her turbaned head inside the door where Madeline lay on the couch and delivered a forgotten message.

"Miss Liney, dat skuyler man he say he's gwine stay ober to de camp so's to be mo' conwenient to his wuk. But he says tell yo' he'll be ober here Saturday night to suppah."

"All right," Madeline responded. She instantly recognized in this arrangement Mann's tactful desire to protect her name. The deserted wife must be shielded from gossip's tarnish. She flinched at the thought but was grateful because she knew the settlement would fall upon an unprotected reputation like a ravening wolf pack.

That same afternoon an intimate friend appeared and was at once ushered into Madeline's presence. India Blair, in a natty gown and toque of dark red, entered the despondent atmosphere like a burst of sunshine and folded Madeline in her comforting arms. With her head on India's shoulder the unhappy wife shed the first relieving tears of her enforced widowhood. It was a tumultuous, healing flood of which she had believed herself incapable.

"I'm having serious trouble at the mill," was India's first coherent remark. She was too tactful to speak of Brett. Instead she talked of her own difficulties. "Matt Crane is not getting on. We – Mother and I – have been caring for him and we're at the breaking point. It's a bad case. Dr. Armstrong probed the cut and removed the steel fragment, but the wound's infected. Matt's getting feverish. I'm terribly anxious about him. If you would only come --."

India's dark eyes finished the sentence. She was determined to lure Madeline into work that would heal both the patient and physician.

"It's blood poison," Madeline decided. "A hard fight may save him but there's no time to lose. I'll go with you at once. If the cut was anywhere but his side there might be hope. As it is I can't tell."

Exactly as India intended, her friend's lifesaving instinct outweighed private trouble.

She packed a suitcase, accompanied India home with Billy-boy and was soon at the sick man's bedside where he raved in delirium. Gentle, frightened Mrs. Blair looked to Madeline for courage as days passed breathless with the fear of impending tragedy. Then the turn came and Matt slept peacefully with his ravings stilled. The danger was over. India took the triumphant physician home Saturday for needed garments. Besides, this was the evening Mann was expected to supper. Sally had done her best for the occasion.

"Baked corn bread what 'u'd melt in yo' mouf," she reported. "An dere's fried chicken, an' squash, an' taters nigh spoiled wid waiting."

They didn't wait long as Mann was even then at the door. But after he greeted the girl lumberjack it is doubtful whether he distinguished potatoes from squash or corn bread from waffles. India wore cloth tinted like gold and flashing with jet. And she herself scintillated with a brilliance of splendid beauty. Her vivid loveliness, her flashing smile, her sparkling wit went to the tallier's head. He forgot the stigma of his past, forgot his vows of prudence, forgot everything but the delight of India's bewildering presence. The virile, fearless, unconventional woman and the clean-souled man were attracted to each other by the power that calls a lion to its mate, the eagle to its other self or the robin of crimson breast to the one of paler hue.

VIII

A Country Ball

A week before the great countryside event – the New Year's Ball – Deb Huff, the Blair's hired girl, admitted Walter Nordyke to the ground floor living room where Mrs. Blair received him.

"I called to see your daughter" the company's bookkeeper told her.

"India is upstairs in the office," Mrs. Blair explained. "She is working on the books."

"With your permission I'll find her," Nordyke said quickly. "I know the way."

With a bound he was up the open stair and entered India's office where he found her bending over books and papers. At his abrupt appearance she looked up in astonishment and immediately stood upright as if waiting for him to state his errand. Her garb was the jaunty suit of corduroy, but her luxuriant mass of nut brown hair was high-coiled adding dignity to her commanding height.

"If you will give me an hour of your time for a drive," he suggested, "I'll tell you what I came to say."

"Impossible," denied the girl lumberjack. "I'm to help Mrs. Brett in Matt Crane's sick room. I should be there now."

"Then," plunged Nordyke, "I am here to request your company for the New Year's dance."

India directed at her suave, black eyed admirer the swift, driven to bay glance of a hunted animal. So this was his mission. She knew her answer must be unhesitatingly prompt and convincing. Nothing on earth would induce her to accompany him anywhere at any time. But to refuse his invitation without an excellent reason meant, in the settlement, a deadly insult. She hated and distrusted the handsome scoundrel with all her soul yet she must be discreet. She must not flagrantly offend. As she desperately cudgeled her wits for some convincing means of escape there came, flash-like, a way out so daring she paled at the thought.

"I'm engaged for the holiday ball," she told him, and waited knowing he would supply the name of her self-elected escort.

Nordyke's sloe black eyes regarded her intently. Then his thin lips smiled with the curious uplift at the corner.

"Permit me to congratulate Forrest Mann on his good fortune," he sneered. "I've learned that procrastination is a deplorable habit. Good night."

He stepped out of the office door and swung gracefully along the ridge path leaving India alone with her triumphant embarrassment. She had rid herself of an undesirable suitor, but she was now at the mercy of the man she was supposed to favor.

If the scaler neglected to ask her company for the dance Nordyke would understand the meaning of her absence. He would guess the riddle. Besides India, abounding with vigorous life, greatly desired to attend the gay affair and have a good time. She was human and good times were few and far between. With head supported on a firm hand she pondered her equivocal situation. Would Forrest Mann invite her to attend the ball? If not --.

The sentence was never finished. Hot blood mounted to India's vivid face like a flame, but her dark eyes were fondly luminous. She believed that her evening's enjoyment was perfectly safe.

That night Donald's continued absence was freely discussed at Steel and Hawley's lumber camp.

"He maybe lit out with a wad of the Company's cash," suggested dare-devil Jim Sprik from his seat by the four-sided fireplace.

"What in hell you talking about?" demanded Hilliker from the midst of his smoke cloud. "Don't you know that Brett never handled the pay roll, you jay-hawk?"

"No, by gorra," substantiated Mike Munshaw. "It's yon blackguard at the sture what fingers the pelf. If ony one skips out wid a bunch o' the boys' pay you'll know his picture and it won't resemble Brett."

"Nordyke bane too sleek: he's ta faller needs a watch on heem," Claus Anderson boldly stated, then subsided when he noticed Stimson's ferret eyes glancing about the circle of faces. Forrest Mann had just entered the room and stood in the background stroking Tam O'Shanter's silky fur when the bush-monkey suddenly entered the discussion.

"Folks that ain't blind kin see through the hole in a grindstun," he shrilled in his queer falsetto. "Most anybody knows Brett lit out and left that handsome wife o' his'n to them that wants her."

"Shut up, you fool," warned Brinkley, but he was too late. Stimson's last words gurgled in his throat as Mann shook him from side to side, then cast him backward across the bench where he sprawled ludicrously on the plank floor. The scaler with face marble white would have followed up his victim but Ben Heald held him back.

"Hit something solid," he told the tally-man. "Don't waste yourself on a bag o' wind."

"You cur," Mann blazed at the roadmaker. "Don't dare defile a woman's name. You beast!"

"You think you're smart, don't you," squeaked Stimson angrily as he rose in a vantage area back of the bench. His weasel-like visage was ashen with rage. "You think you're a swell, do you. You're up here in the timber for your health, ain't you, Mr. Forrest Mann? 'Tain't everybody has such a fit name, is it? Looks like you had it made a purpose so's to keep your other clean. It's --."

"Shut up," roared Brinkley. "You got what was coming to you. If Mann hadn't knocked you galley west the rest of us would have made you swallow your teeth."

By this time the scaler had passed out of the bunkroom to a small apartment in the cook house which had been converted to his use. It had formerly been Long Jim's store room. Here Mann kept his tally books, helped Bob Stray with his studies, and slept. Bob was already at his school books by a table he had contrived out of a barrel. By the light of a kerosene lamp the scaler copied his day's work then helped Bob with his reading and figures.

"Time for you to turn in, my boy," Mann finally told his pupil. "And it's time for me to turn out." He stood up, slipped into a heavy fur coat, then pausing with his hand on the door latch, reminded his companion: "If anyone raps at the door remember we are both asleep and the bolt shot."

"All right," his mate answered. "Nobody gets in but you," Bob assured the scaler without lifting his eyes from the absorbing page.

Silently Mann passed out of the deserted kitchen and strode down a logging road to the Blair skidways. Having reached the spot he took up watch in a nearby grove of dwarf pine. The night was black with lowering storm clouds and thick with a soft snow that muffled sound. It was an ideal time for the diabolical work of a log spiker; but an hour dragged by, then another dropped its minutes like beads of eternities before the self-appointed guard received his reward.

Suddenly there passed him in the clogging snow a horse and cutter that loomed unreal, shadowy in the intense darkness. The driver stopped by the farthest pile of Blair logs and alighted. Instantly Mann sprang forward intent upon identifying the late traveler. His act was a tactical blunder. The stranger being warned, flung himself back in his seat, struck his horse a furious blow with the whip and the whole vanished like the figment of a dream. Trailing the rig was useless. Once in the beaten highway the interloper was safe, and snow was erasing his tracks.

Was it possible this man was the log spiker, and that he came from a distance? The thought was maddening. Mann supposed he was to deal with someone hired on the spot. This adventure directed his suspicion into new channels. With lighted matches he examined the place where the phantom horse and sleigh had stopped by the Blair skidway. The tracks were fast filling with snow and merged further on with ruts of the logging bunks. At the highway the night driver turned east which indicated he was a farmer, and no farmer would spike logs. Puzzled and disturbed Mann slowly returned to his room thinking of many things.

"Just why," he mused, "did Stimson accuse me of adopting an alias? What has the fellow heard?" The perplexing question lasted him until he reached the battened door of his room and was admitted by his watchful pupil.

"Someone did try the door," reported Bob, "and it frightened me. He came shortly after you left. I wouldn't speak, just snored and he went away. Afterward my eyes popped wide open as an owl's. I couldn't sleep."

"Well, you can sleep now," Mann told him. "The locked door turned the trick. It's all right."

At last came the evening of the great holiday ball. In the big dance hall above the Company's store bracket lights with reflectors shone on the waxed floor and brilliantly lighted the gay scene. On a raised platform a country orchestra tuned up violins while by ones and twos and groups jovial guests trooped up the wide stair. Men wore every manner of apparel from the gaudy mackinaw to store clothes. Young, middle aged and elderly women occupied the benches that lined the walls. They were dressed in faded finery or new costumes contrived for the occasion. The few town's women, however, formed an exclusive circle and wore correct toilettes that alone set them apart. Immediately the floor filled with dancers and became a whirl of bright color and smiling faces. Hod Elwin, handsomely dressed in new attire, stood on the orchestra platform and shouted the dance call in a half chant.

"Balance with the lady at your right hand," he intoned, "and swing with the girl behind you."

Laughingly the dancers obeyed while wallflowers watched the later arrivals – Ridman with his pretty wife, Ed Dalton, Nordyke, handsome and distinguished in appearance. His ebon black hair and eyes contrasted with his white skin and his thin lips smiled with the curious uplift that was almost a sneer. At his side walked a man who was the instant target of all eyes. He was a tall commanding figure with a fine head fearlessly poised. His thick hair was light brown and his frank, wide-open eyes were gentian blue and laughter-filled even when his strongly molded features were in repose. Like all men of the period who were not fully bearded he wore a heavy mustache that added vastly to his fine appearance. This distinguished stranger was presently known to be Robert Floyd, the new manager, who was to fill Brett's vacancy.

Exited interest in the new manager had not diminished when an entering couple drew public attention. At the stair head appeared Forrest Mann and India Blair. Mann, in city attire, looked every inch an urbanite who handled books instead of logs. India was smilingly radiant. Her cream silk, trimmed and sashed with cardinal, exactly suited her brilliant beauty and flashing eyes. In some manner known only to a clever woman she had solved her problem.

Being an active lumber dealer, familiar with every phase of the business made her a prime favorite with lumberjacks. Her hearty, almost boyish manner and utter lack of self-consciousness put the shyest woodsman at his ease. He could talk logs with her as with another lumberjack, and she was in constant demand. Her silken garments awed no one. Every young man of the settlement, including her own mill crew, sought a dance with the girl mill owner as the great room became a kaleidoscopic galaxy of color and resonant with life. Nordyke and Robert Floyd stood by the bandstand observing the throng while Hod Elwin bellowed above the uproar of music and shuffling feet the terse command: "Couples pass through and down the hall!"

Instantly the dancers came forward in a double column like a joyous parade. Among them was Lily May. Her painstakingly crimped, down hanging hair was fair as flax, and her childishly beautiful face was delicate as a tea rose. Her innocent, sky blue eyes sparkled like twin stars and her red lips parted over teeth like pearls.

"Pretty as a Dresden china doll," noted Nordyke. "She's a wild flower of the woods that will turn to weeds. They don't last."

Behind Lily May swept forward dark-eyed, imperious India Blair. If Lily was a wild flower India was a flaming orchid. Her gown with its flashes of red sharply contrasted, like the wearer, with poor Lily's faded delaine, unskillfully made and of magenta tint. No two women could be more unalike yet both were superbly beautiful.

When the set ended Nordyke carried out his design of securing India for the next dance which was to be a waltz. Ladies carried no dance cards but to refuse a suppliant for a number not already taken was, again, by settlement standard, an unforgivable insult. As the bookkeeper murmured his request India gazed at him in cool denial. To be guided through the maze in Nordyke's arms inspired her with loathing. She was not of the meek, pliant sort nor lacking in resource so she swiftly extricated herself from the dilemma.

"Excuse me," she said with a brilliant smile, "but I dance this with Bob Stray." Whereupon she whirled that astonished youth into the vortex of swirling couples.

In spite of Bob's awkward attempt at the unfamiliar steps India kept him valiantly at his task. She was a fine dancer with keen delight in the rhythmic movement, so she deftly evaded her young partners blundering feet and wickedly enjoyed both Nordyke's chagrin and her escape from his hated embrace. Nordyke, inwardly swearing, turned for consolation to Lily May. Here his request amounted to delicate flattery. The unsophisticated country girl accepted the attention of Steel and Hawley's representative as if he were a prince. She assumed an ease of manner far removed from her mental condition of painful shyness. Her feet, usually nimble, now stumbled, but her partner held her firmly in a clasp that set her romantic heart to wildly beating. At the end of the waltz the handsome bookkeeper remained at the girl's side and managed a monologue since the shy, ignorant child could find nothing to say. When presently Nordyke asked permission to see her home she lifted china blue eyes to his face in wonder at her triumph, and gave an affirmative answer in a low monosyllable.

Once more Nordyke sought the favor of a dance with Blair but this time India was actually promised to Robert Floyd, the newly arrived manager, who had laughingly purchased a ball ticket and joined the festivities.

"Curse her for a proud upstart," was Nordyke's mental reservation. "She'll pay for this in expensive coin."

Several times during the night Lily May's white rose beauty was emphasized by the Mephistophelian comeliness of the bookkeeper in different sets. Moreover she was his partner at the richly laden supper table in the boarding house across the way. Lily ate in silence, but her pale cheeks bloomed and her eyes were twin stars. Assuredly she had made a notable conquest.

That night when Forrest Mann started with his partner for the home drive he wondered why he had permitted himself to seek danger. He was thoroughly aware that his sentiment toward the girl at his side was the grand passion realized at the dinner with Madeline. Because of his hidden life he believed his love a crime. Since then he meant to avoid India's enchanting presence when not compelled by circumstances to confer with her on matters concerning the tally of her logs. These rare occasions were to be his reward for renunciation. And during their duration he would school himself to repression. He dared not tax his love beyond endurance. With soul hunger growing, the desire to possess the object of his devotion increasing, he was forced to guard his every act and tone. India must not suspect the truth. Her peace of mind must not be disturbed.

Now he found himself in the great moonless night with the woman he adored. Her warm young beauty was so near her breath swept his cheek as she turned to speak. He could visualize her as she had appeared in the lighted hall – a glowing, flashing creature of exquisite life. His whole being ached to speak his love and take her in his arms, but honor forced the words back in his throat. He was polished marble enclosing a flame. When he handed her from the sleigh and accompanied her to the office door his handclasp was of steel. Even his voice chilled with self-mastering emotion.

As India settled in her room for a half hour's exquisite reverie she wondered at the sense of disappointment haunting her otherwise slated mind. It had been an easy matter to secure her desired escort for the evening. While discussing the holiday event in Matt Crane's room she had expressed a wish to attend and Mann instantly offered to gratify her desire. He was discreet and practical, but India's keen intuition revealed the scaler's secret – the blissful knowledge of his devotion. Why had he failed to give her assurance of the truth? A murmured "I love you" would have perfected her evening. It would have been a crowning joy. With the simplicity of a fool Mann thought he might approach fire and not be burned. Worse: he who would have defended India with his life had not guarded her against himself.

"I love him," she murmured as she uncoiled her wealth of dark brown hair and braided it for the night. "I love him," she repeated with her eyes soft as velvet. "And some time I'll make him tell me – what – I – already – know."

IX

Madeline Brett Finds Employment

Matt Crane's critical illness diverted Madeline Brett's overburdened mind from the horror that almost drove her mad. After he became convalescent she turned with zest to her books. By indulging in exhausting study she made sleep a certainty. Her old school and college books joined the pile on the reading table because she intended to teach and earn her living, therefore a preparatory brushing up of each subject was essential. The sale of her husband's driving team and his quarter's unpaid salary would support her small family until spring. After that there were summer schools in the settlement which were her hope of employment. Medical practice was out of the question. The poverty ridden settlement would yield nothing worthwhile to a self-taught physician, so she studied medicine as a recreation and delved deeply into text books for a more serious purpose.

She was thus occupied before her book piled table when Sally one morning admitted Robert Floyd.

"Like everyone else," said he in his deep musical bass, "I've come to you when in trouble." His frank blue eyes were brilliant with vitality. His vigorous personality dispelled morbidness. In his exuberant presence life appeared sane and normal. His hearty handclasp, tingling with energy, suddenly dispersed Madeline's lowering clouds and brought her to a sun-flooded earth.

"I'm here to ask a favor," he confessed. "The case is this: I have but one near relative - relative – a son. As I can't think of taking him to board with me at Jobbin's, I was wondering if you could accept him as a member of your family. I will gladly pay for his board."

Madeline gasped with amazement. What would she do with a rollicking boy? How would Sally like the added care? The lad might be unruly, noisy, disagreeable. Yet the money paid for his accommodation would do much to solve her financial problems.

"You forgot to mention the child's age," she reminded him.

Floyd laughed outright. "You're seeing visions of a turbulent infant in knickers," he guessed. "Here's Phil to speak for himself." From a pocket he produced a photograph and handed it across the table to Madeline who saw pictured a fifteen year old lad, slender and delicate in appearance but with the same frank countenance and mirthful eyes of the father.

"His mother died at his birth," Floyd explained in softened tones. "He never had the right start. His health has always been a matter of grave anxiety. I sincerely hope you will let him come and give him the benefit of the woods, Sally's cooking and your care.

He's being boarded in Chicago. Say the word and I'll have him here by Saturday."

Madeline's eyes were fixed on the bright young face smiling at her from the photograph. "Suppose," she thought, "that my child had lived while I died." Her heart was won to Phil's cause.

"You may send for the boy, Mr. Floyd," she consented. "He's welcome."

Phil's doting parent departed well satisfied. He had accomplished more than securing a home for his son. During his calls at the former manager's home to examine the records, Madeline's forlorn condition, her amazing beauty and her courage wrung his heart with compassion. He tried to think out some plan for her welfare; then Phil's urgent need of ozone and good food furnished the answer.

That afternoon Mrs. Swisher flounced into the Brett kitchen and settled herself for an advice-giving interview.

"I hear you're going to apply for our school," she began in her quick, abrupt utterance as Madeline seated herself by the caller.

"Yes, I am," admitted the deserted wife. "I understand the present teacher intends to leave. When he does I shall apply for the vacancy."

"Well, you won't have long to wait or I miss my guess," declared Mrs. Swisher. "Percy Tinkham is driv to his wits end. A pusson might's well tackle a passel o' lunatics as them three terrors. Rast Quick's the devil's own child, and Bob Davitt ain't a peg behind. As for Sim Parsons his ma says them boys has swore to put you out if you try the school. She thought you oughta be warned."

Into Madeline's handsome face streamed the fighting blood of the old South. Her dark eyes flashed. "If I take the school I'll teach it to the finish," she recklessly promised.

"No woman has kept that school sence the terrors growed up," stated Mrs. Swisher ominously. "They're a bad lot."

"At least I shall attend the teacher's examination held at Agache next week," insisted Madeline. "If I pass requirements I shall ask for the school."

"Then you're not the sort I took you for," Mrs. Swisher frankly admitted. "I reckoned you'd be easy scared, but folks can't be judged by their looks. For my part I think you're a fool to be pestered by them young savages, but I wish you luck."

At the teacher's examination Mr. John Burch, county superintendent, presided. He was lean and tall with a parchment covered visage while an atmosphere of learning exhaled from the black frock suit that flapped about his august person. Madeline discovered that the dreaded ordeal was a matter of eighth grade simplicity. Her competitors were a few young girls, ill at ease and falsely encouraged by rural teachers to attempt the impossible. Among them was Lily May dressed in her faded delaine, painfully apprehensive and horribly frightened. Mrs. Brett's heart overflowed with pity for the child-woman. Within her protecting arms Lily mopped her overflowing blue eyes while her yellow hair tumbled about her slender shoulders.

"Oh, I can't answer the questions, Mrs. Brett," she wailed. "I never heard of roots and Singapore. I was never told of tenses or infinitives. Ma will be so ashamed of me. What shall I do?"

"Study hard another term or two," Madeline told her. "After that you'll wonder why you worried."

The two returned home in the Brett rig back of Brett's well matched team of bays, now the property of Robert Floyd but often placed at Madeline's service. At a side road near the Brett farm Lily alighted with a happier face and hurried to her father's log cabin. She had comforted herself with the old-world solace – she looked forward to success. Besides, her new friend might teach the summer school. Lily rejoiced.

Armed with her teacher's certificate, Madeline next visited Jud Coon, district school director. He lived in a mud-plastered log cabin with a decrepit barn at the rear flanked by straw stacks where huddled lean cattle and hogs and foraging hens. He had cut his patch of farm from the wilderness but the virgin soil provided plenty of hog and hominy diet, so the family flourished. Her knock at the battened door was answered by Sarah Coon, untidy and evidently unwashed, but with her sun-faded hair elaborately crimped. She had seen Madeline at the religious meetings and knew who asked for her father.

"Dad's in the woodlot," she told the applicant. "I'll call him. Walk in."

The room Madeline entered was the usual settlement combination of kitchen, dining room and parlor. The spare bed, covered by a rising-sun quilt, gave one corner of the room an air of elegance. Mrs. Coon, rail-like and with babe in her arms, stepped forward to welcome the caller and offer a chair.

"Yes'm, the baby's well," she assured Madeline. "We just has to keep well. There ain't no money to be sick an' we couldn't afford to bury ourselves if we died. Funerals is costly."

Her pessimistic remarks ended with the appearance of Jud Coon who verified his wife's claim to poverty. Flapping rags were confined about his meager waist by a bit of rope. His thin face retreated back of straggling whiskers and an old oil cloth cap topped off his unkempt hair.

His manner, however, was important to the last degree. He surmised Mrs. Brett's errand and was alive to the fact that he had the power to give or withhold employment.

"Know what sorter school this is?" he asked in a shrill falsetto after a brief discussion.

"Yes, I've been informed of it," smiled Madeline.

"Then," said the director, changing his quid of home grown to the opposite cheek, "if you're lookin' for trouble at twenty six dollars a month I'm willing."

"Very well," agreed Madeline. "I'm glad of the work and ready to teach at a minute's notice."

Saturday morning ushered in a furious snow storm, but at six o'clock there sounded sleigh bells, the door flew open and Robert Floyd presented to Madeline the slender, laughing-eyed boy of the photograph. Before she could speak her hands were impulsively grasped in cold fingers and a boyish voice proclaimed:

"Here's Floyd junior, Mrs. Brett, and he's half starved."

"And half frozen," laughed Floyd senior. "If I'd known this blizzard was on the way I'd have had him wait at Hickory Vale."

"Your hands are ice, Phil," cried Madeline. "And supper's ready. Have Sam stable your horses," she told the elder Floyd, "while you eat."

"I believe," was Robert Floyd's form of acceptance as he gazed about the cozy rooms with their bright lights, glowing hearths and delectable whiffs of Sally's cooking, "that I was born under a lucky star."

Phil's lively interest in everything about him added zest to the evening meal. From the moment of his arrival the atmosphere cleared and brightened. The whole place seemed filled with the wholesome magnetism of Floyd junior's presence.

Later in the evening the new manager placed a generous advance for his son's board on the reading table. "Phil is fortunate," he declared. "I hope he'll appreciate the favor you've shown him."

"Now don't you worry about that, Father-Bob," assured Phil. "Your son's chuck full of gratitude already."

Sally, who had rebelled at the advent of a boy in her kitchen, expressed modified opinions while she washed the supper dishes.

"Nebber in m' bo'n days did I see a boy git away wid sich helpings o' puddin'," commented the flattered cook.

"I could of et mo' puddin' myse'f," regretted Sam.

"I nebber see yo' so full dat you's willin' to quit," stated Sam's dusky wife as she reached for a dish towel. "Yo' allus act like yo' was born hongry."

"I was," confirmed Sam. "I allus hatter eat hoecake made outen chicken feed till Miss Liney's pa buy me, an' abber sence it seems I cain't git enough o' white man's vittles."

Steel and Hawley's lumberjacks were forced to quit work because of the blizzard. Teamsters were blinded. Swift driven snow cut like points of steel.

The men's snow-dusted clothing froze into suits of mail. So Brinkley let his men quit at quarter time in the afternoon.

"Ain't seen a storm like this sence I cut logs on the Muskegon," squeaked Haywire Hank as he removed his snow-clogged shoe-packs.

"You'll see three days o' this and ten foot snow drifts," prophesied Jet Lowney.

"Anyhow, we'll log that forty if we have to tunnel," said Brinkley by the fireplace, hands clasped back of his head and his swarthy face red with the heat of blazing hemlock.

"By gar," suddenly exclaimed Jules Deveraux, looking about the bunk room, "tat wizzle o' a Stimson mus' a poked hisself in a snow bank. He ain't come. What he stop for?"

With an uneasy start Mann verified the Frenchman's statement.

"Tampering with the Blair logs," he decided, and hastily passed out into the storm. With head bent to the blast he started toward the Blair skidways and a quarter mile away he came face to face with the man he sought. As the scaler suspiciously stared at the lithe bush-monkey Stimson's weasel-like countenance was overspread by a snow-crusted grin.

"He's succeeded," thought Mann who had supposed Stimson too cowardly for the deed. Without a word he passed the swamper and tried to track him to the skidway that had received the bolt. As he proceeded the man's tracks filled with drifting snow. The raging tempest swept the way to a smooth surface. One course was open. Each log under suspicion must be marked. With his tally pencil he accordingly made a black cross on the exposed ends, then he returned to camp.

Long Jim's supper that night was a feast of dried apple mince pies, cookies and dried- apple sauce. Guy's heavy red head bobbed and swayed as with his red mouth a-grin he shambled hither and thither with extra helpings of food. The hearty meal, accompanied by pint cups of boiling tea, put the lumberjacks in rare good humor. On their return to the bunk house one and another broke into rough, riotous song, and a loud demand ensued for Jet Lowney and his fiddle.

Immediately the dark, wiry fiddler, accompanied by big, blond Tom Bordon, tuned up and swung into the air of a popular lumbering song which the lumberjacks caught up until eighty men were singing with gusto and noisy abandon. Many of the crew had excellent voices and their lusty rhythm was inspiring as they shouted out the lines:

> "You may talk about your sweethearts, your pleasures and your plays; But you don't think of us poor shanty boys working here as slaves. We enjoy no better pastime than to hunt the buck and doe, So we'll range the wild woods over and once more a-lumbering go."

Marking time with stamping feet, the lumberjacks repeated the last line over and over:

> "And once more a-lumbering go, and once more a-lumbering go, We'll range the wild woods over and once more a-lumbering go."

The song ended when the violins ceased the tune and changed to the accent strains of 'The Highland Fling.'

"McDougal! McDougal!" yelled the crew, and in response a huge Scotchman in mackinaw plaid advanced to the middle of the long floor and with unsuspected lightness of foot, reeled off the flinging, swaying steps of his country's dance. Far down the length of the bunk house swung the big lumberjack to bursts of applause. After that the dance became general. Men in bright hued shirts with brilliant scarfs about their waists formed the figures of a quadrille at the shouted direction of Hod Elwin.

"First 'lady' swing with the right hand gent!" yelled Hod as the violins scraped and twanged the air of 'The Girl I Left Behind Me,' and dancing lumberjacks sung and whistled the refrain.

"That's it Bob; give me your lily white paw! Now, Bill, dance like a lady. Not that way, you galoot, do it pretty," admonished Rube Kinney as he good-naturedly grinned his way down the line. The next man swinging in the reel was Stimson. He now shot out his foot as the scaler passed intending to trip him in revenge for this recent chastisement; but by chance he caught the next dancer and Jim Sprik measured his length on the plank floor.

"Damn you!" Sprik shouted, scrambling upright. Mann, however, understood the meaning of Stimson's act and jerked him aside from Sprik's dangerous onslaught.

"Curse you," Stimson shrilled. "Let me alone and go to the nigger where you belong."

While Stimson bleached with anger at Mann's interference, Sprik blackened with fury. He lurched a blow at Stimson that landed by default on Haywire Hank. That long jointed, inoffensive lover of cats, being assailed without cause, struck back in self-defense.

"Come on, Davitt," Sprik yelled to Bat Davitt, father of the school ruffian. "We'll lick the hull outfit."

At that the dance turned into a free for all fight. Men who had offended Sprik or Davitt were singled out for battle. Friends of these sprang to their defense. Meanwhile Mann caught Stimson by his scrawny throat and hissed in this ear: "Dare to repeat that infamous word and I'll send you up for log-spiking."

The threat was out. Mann had thrown discretion to the wind and had shown his hand to the enemy. Stimson glared but his visage resembled a corpse. With a quick twist he broke loose and wriggled past the fight. Brinkley was loudly shouting for order but the contestants were deep in the joy of conflict.

Hilliker, a powerful man of temperate habits, has been selected by Sprik for this reason. And Jim's accumulated booze helped Hilliker to easily hold his own. Davitt, the local pugilist, had engaged Haywire Hank as the latter was a man of peace with the reputation of being a coward. Over the combatants rolled, clenched and bit. Friends of each joined the spectators and bet on the fight. Sprik managed to snap his teeth on Hilliker's thumb and held it in jaws set like a vise. It was a successful maneuver, but Long Jim secured a frying pan in the kitchen and with the handle of this remarkable instrument pried Jim's teeth apart and released his victim.

"Now finish him, Dan" Mike Munshaw encouraged his friend.

"Stop them!" commanded Brinkley. But Hilliker, maddened by pain fought vindictively while Davitt made short work of Haywire Hank. Then to show the completeness of his victory he grabbed Tam O'Shanter, who had taken refuge on an upper bunk and hurled the pet cat at his owner's head. The insult goaded Hank to unexpected fury.

"By Judas," he squeaked, "I'm just getting mad!"

With a leap he was on the camp bully landing blows like the stroke of a flail. His had a yard reach and the grip of a gorilla. Frenzy lent him miraculous power. No one might abuse his cat and go free. So he administered a thrashing to the camp pugilist that left nothing to be desired.

"By gol," Hank squeaked in his mixed bass and treble, "I did lick him. An' I always thought if I found a man I could lick I'd never quit licking him. But I did lick him and I did quit, an' Long Jim had no call to help me out with no darned frying pan either."

"You fellows may get your discharge when Floyd hears of this," Brinkley warned the combatants. But his voice held a note of quiet satisfaction."

X

A District School

Weeks glided by with few incidents of note. Mann and Stimson watched each other with the result that the Blair logs were secure from the latter, but the scaler's life, had he known it, was in constant peril. India Blair had ordered the logs peeled that Mann marked with a black cross. As a result bolts were found driven deep in four of the thick barked timbers. When India sent the tallier a report of this treachery he conferred with her in her office.

"What does all this mean?" India asked, her face pale with anxiety. "Who is trying to ruin us by frightening my workmen? They intend the men shall quit and leave the mill idle. It's a subtle scheme. Who's behind it?"

Mann regarded her thoughtfully. For a moment he was tempted to relate his encounter with the swamper, then reconsidered.

"I know one man who is guilty," he finally admitted. "There may be others, but I have no proof."

"You know the man?" cried India. Her dark eyes questioned.

"He's the last one you'd suspect," said the scaler, "because he's a coward and has no apparent motive. Until I have proof of his crime the name had better remain unspoken. But knowing this much simplifies the problem. I hope you're willing to trust my discretion."

"I am," cried India. Her tone was eloquent of absolute faith in her champion. Had he not been blinded by a sense of his own unworthiness he'd have known her trust was founded on the wisest of human instincts – love. But the banked fire of his own passion was ready to burst in flame and he doubted his strength to conceal his real sentiment for the owner of Blair's mill.

He rose to go. "I must go home and checkup my tally for today. Good night."

Across India's troubled mind swept a sharp realization of the danger Mann incurred in her service.

"Promise me you'll protect yourself," she cried out in a voice that shook with fear. "The criminal would destroy you because of your suspicion. He'd stop at nothing." The hand Mann held in parting trembled.

"India," he said, using her given name for the first time, "I am glad to serve you whatever the cost. It is the one pleasure of a barren life. The danger is nothing, so don't worry. And, good-by."

With an effort he controlled his surge to remain and speak of other topics than criminals, and so passed out into the night. Within her office India stood a long time in blissful reverie.

"He loves me," she exulted. "He loves me yet won't yet speak. I wonder why."

Long she puzzled over the world old problem. "Next time," she declared, "he shall say the word I long to hear, that is my right to hear – and answer." Her strong face flamed from throat to temple, yet she had no cause for shame. She craved an open avowal of the love she had won. She willed that Forrest Mann should utter the love phrases that would join their lives. So she loved and waited.

At the Brett home Robert Floyd dropped in for one of his frequent evening calls; and from his great coat pocket he extracted a bright eyed animal with fur of fluffy golden brown which he placed on the floor at Madeline's feet.

"There were one too many of the pups at Jobbin's," he explained, "so he sent this one to Phil. If he's a nuisance I can easily take him back."

"The fuzzy darling," cried Madeline. "Send him back? Never! We're grateful to you and Mr. Jobbin. We'll keep him of course."

"Thank you, Mrs. Brett," Phil said gratefully. "I've always wanted a collie, but they're not a city dog. They're awfully delicate and usually die."

When Phil introduced his waddling pet to the kitchen both Aunt Sally and the family cat manifested lively disapproval.

"Lan' sakes," ejaculated the turbaned negress, "w'at yo' fetch dat lil beas' ter pester me fo'?"

Sukey, the Maltese cat, began a diagonal retreat then bounded to security on top of a dish cupboard just as Sam entered with an armful of morning kindling.

"Glory, dat's a dog," he exclaimed in delight. "Been a wantin' a coon dog. Woods am chock full o' the fines' coon dat ebber stole corn."

"Humph," snorted Sally. "Dat ar handful o' ha'r looks heap like a coon dog, do he? I'd catch jes' as much coon wid Sukey, an' mo' too. If I don' miscalculate yo' bettah put dat huntin' dog in a cage or Suke'll eat him up."

Bruno, as Phil named his collie, rapidly developed an astonishing ability to look after himself. His abnormal growth was illustrated daily by his increasing difficulty in adjusting his silky self into his early sleeping quarters – one of Sam's old hats. Bruno was puzzled. With painstaking care he would thrust his front feet in the hat and try to curl down. But despite careful calculations his hindquarters spilled over! Patiently he renewed his effort by backing into the hat, but to his disgust his forequarters were out in the cold. Again and again he repeated the process until wearied by his unsolvable problem the pudgy beast dropped asleep with the end of himself in the hat that chance dictated.

"Dat ar dog got fuss rate qualities," admitted Sally after one of Bruno's disagreements with the old felt hat. "He's a determined critter, dat's suah."

The collie's advent completed Phil's happiness. He attended the district school, helped Sam after school hours and Saturdays, and won the black man's delighted assistance in trapping. But school under the management of Percy Tinkham was not to be classed with unmixed blessings. Robert Floyd, however, wished his son to gain strength of character and health, so he favored a certain amount of roughing it by way of contact with the toughs that terrorized

District No. 4. Phil, being tactful and pleasant, avoided trouble for a time and gained amusement.

His presence in the Brett home routed the abnormal and kept Madeline's brooding mind healthily sane. He was a wholesome interest and his health and comfort became her chief thought. He in turn served his hostess with untiring devotion. His attachment later was her source of courage under trying circumstances. Phil, himself, was herald of the tidings that sent her to the torture chamber of a district school.

"Mr. Coon sent word you were to begin teaching right away," announced Phil, having arrived from school at an unexpected hour. "He wants you to start tomorrow morning."

"How can that be?" Madeline asked.

"Because Mr. Tinkham had a block out this morning, and he quit."

"A block out," exclaimed Madeline. "What's that?"

"Cordwood," explained Phil. "Mr. Tinkham asked the boys to bring in enough wood to last out the week because he don't like to soil his hands. So last night and this morning they carried in twelve cords. When Mr. Tinkham came to open the school the room was solid full to the door. It made him mad. He took the stage for home, and Mr. Coon says you may begin your term tomorrow morning."

"Very well," agreed Madeline with a shiver of apprehension, "I'll be on hand."

Mr. Coon concerned himself but little over the succession of instructors. He with his son removed the block wood from the settlement hall of learning, then turned his ragged back on the whole affair and let the new teacher shift for herself.

Accompanied by Phil, Madeline walked along the forest road to begin her first day's work. She had desired an outlet for her energies and suddenly found it. Every settlement dweller awaited the result. Could a woman master the element that evicted Percy Tinkham? They thought not; and said so.

As the teacher neared the familiar building pupils, bearing dinner pails, converged from every direction. Among them she recognizes Rast Quick, black browed and surly, Bob Davitt, the reckless rowdy, and Sim Parsons of beanpole dimensions and fishy eye.

Davitt, with his cloth cap at a rakish angle, was in the lead. Quick came next, slightly limping from a onetime broken leg, and Sim lurched forward whistling with hands in pockets. He stared curiously at the new instructor from under low brows and above a nose so flattened it spread on his freckled countenance. Madeline's heart sank at sight of the Three Terrors. That they were permitted to trouble her – or others – with their demoralizing presence was due to the fact that expulsion from a district school was never practiced. Teachers were supposed to master the situation or be conquered. So Madeline summoned her courage, joined a group of admiring girls and entered the square log building used for both church and school.

Within the building awaited her some twenty children of all ages who circled the box stove where Jim Coon had started a roaring fire. One of these was Zoe Higbee, a country belle, clad in a bright hued alpaca. Her thick, black hair was done up in what she imagined was a stunning coiffure. She greeted Madeline with a nod of condescension then turned to the big boys in the doorway. She was of the type that infests about every district school – boy crazy and indifferent to books. In fact it was Zoe Higbee who incited the terrors to lawless acts and they strove for her favor.

Back of her desk-table Madeline rang a hand bell for order. Instantly there was a scramble for choice seats. At a word all subsided but the Triple Terrors, and they stood obstinately at a center seat near the rear. A glance showed Madeline that Phil was in possession.

"This is our desk," Bob Davitt explained. "We three always sets right here."

Madeline's wits worked with lightening rapidity. To permit these boys to join forces was death to discipline, yet to scatter the insurgents was to court disaster. Directly across from this seat sat Zoe Higbee, Sarah Coon and Kate Roth. The friendly eyes of Lily May and Em Jobbin anxiously watched the approaching crisis. Phil, however, settled the matter by sliding his books from the wooden desk and stepping out of the seat and the dispute. The teacher accepted his cue of peace diplomacy and, without comment, opened the morning session with song. This was a happy diversion since music had little place in the children's home and Percy Tinkham had not favored singing because he couldn't sing. Now a familiar patriotic song directed by Madeline's splendid soprano cleared the air before she organized her classes.

District school work in the log cabin period was mainly covered by the three R's. Reading classes from the ambitious Fifth Reader to the lowly primer came first in order. Consequently the older pupils lined up from Madeline's desk to the water pail at the door. Lily May's fair head and pretty face was next to the teacher and when she read her lines Madeline was astonished at her perfect execution. Phil followed with more vigor but less art. Zoe Higbee mumbled her verse then passed the book to Bob Davitt. According to her plans she invariably secured a place between two boys and was content without absorbing knowledge. This was true of Quick and Davitt who read almost from memory.

Sign Post, as Parsons was known, read in Sander's Fourth. At least he held the book and helplessly eyed the offending page that treated of Labor which might have been an uncongenial subject. Finally he hunched one shoulder and laboriously proclaimed, "Labor – is – rest – from – the sorrows – that – greet – us." The last two words of the line after long scrutiny and muttered spelling were spoken as if labor acted on the human system as an irritant. Billy Duff, next in line, suffered from an abnormally developed sense of humor, added to extreme nervousness. Sim's rendition of Labor affected Billy disastrously. He clutched his nose in a grip of despair and his blue eyes filled with tears of suppressed mirth. Awe of the lady teacher intensified his predicament until he burst into hysterical laughter. The entire school looked up in lively or dismayed interest. Percy Tinkham would have whirled the victim of ill-timed merriment into a corner and left him standing as a warning to offenders, so they breathlessly awaited Madeline's judgement.

The new teacher, by violent effort, suppressed her own desire to laugh as Billy broke out in gulps and gurgles, attempting an apology.

"Te – teacher," he gasped, "I c- can't gug – gug – gug help it."

"Suppose," whispered Madeline to him, "that you go outdoors and stop thinking of Sim. I'm sure you'll be able to read when you come back."

Immensely relieved at the turn of affairs Billy obeyed. When he returned from a contemplation of the snow world he read his stanza with only a few diminishing giggles.

The remaining days of the week passed quietly. The Triple Terrors, named by Phil, The Triangle, were in no haste to renew their winter sport of annoying the instructor. Rast Quick was patient. He planned leisurely and accomplished thoroughly. Deceived, Madeline began to feel encouraged. She believed the boys might be reclaimed. Had she known the Triangles energies were being expended on hatching up trouble for David Johnathan she might have reserved her opinion.

As usual the Brett household attended the Sunday evening service for Madeline wished to diminish comment on her enforced widowhood by showing a brave front to the neighborhood. If Donald Brett returned these people need never know she believed herself deserted. Besides, the circuit rider's vigorous militant language inspired her with strength. His flame and fire eloquence roused her to heights of exaltation, and here she saw kindly faces and felt less forlorn. India, for one, greeted her with welcoming smile and clinging hands. The two friends occupied their accustomed seat. India, garbed in her favorite gold-brown with a scarlet wing in her turban, was radiant. The happiness of that last evening in her office with Mann gave luster to her dark eyes, and she was conscious that the scaler was seated directly behind them. Across the aisle Nordyke, perfectly groomed, held one side of a hymn book with Robert Floyd as the congregation sang: "The dying thief rejoiced to see that fountain in his day."

Mrs. Brett's magnificent voice threaded the slow measure like a silver chime, and many stopped singing to listen.

"She's not grieving much for Brett," whispered Ann Groot, a hatchet-faced gossip, to Mrs. Parsons. But Sim's mother was craning her neck to catch a glimpse of the beautiful singer who was now the much discussed teacher of District Number Four.

The energetic preacher, whose influence in the settlement was unbounded, began his sermon. He had selected the story of Daniel in the lion's den. His voice during the reading was impressive. It was even more emphatic as he for the last time delivered the words of his text: "Be ye not afraid of sudden fear, neither of the desolation of the wicked when it cometh."

At the last word David Johnathan, to the amazement of his hearers, dropped from sight through the gaping floor. Nothing but a black chasm remained. The big circuit rider had disappeared like a pebble in a murky pool. Astonishment held each one spellbound until Robert Floyd and Brinkley stepped to the opening. A hand lamp revealed a cellar deep cavity beneath two sawed floors – the platform and plank flooring. Nothing else. The vigorous parson was not in the rude basement. As Brinkley lowered himself to further search the excavation the outer door opened to admit the missing preacher. In one powerful hand he held Bob Davitt by the collar. With quick strides he advanced to the front, plumped his captive in a conspicuous seat, then resumed his discourse at the point of interruption and finished his sermon in front of instead of at the rear of his desk, and with one eye on his prisoner.

The episode was Rast Quick's revenge. He had planned David Johnathan's downfall, but he had not expected the circuit rider to instantly grasp the situation and his lieutenant. When Bob Davitt, at a signal, pulled away the supports under their improvised trap door David Johnathan was quick enough to catch him red-handed.

Once only the settlement preacher paused in his evening's flow of eloquence and then it was to seize his captive in contemplated flight. This added zest to his discourse which was unduly lengthened, but it held not a word concerning the Triple Terrors and their trick unless his organ-deep bass suggested it in the closing hymn: "My soul be on thy guard."

Two figures detached themselves from the congregation and passed out of luminous moonlight into the enveloping forest where a robe-filled vehicle received them and a word sent the horses speeding inland. When the rig, without bells, slipped into splotches of light the girl's hair gleamed like spun gold.

"My beautiful darling," the man whispered. "My white lily."

And the horse without bells to give a gay accompaniment to hoof beats, sped over sparkling fields of snow or paced slowly under the shadow of the forest.

"My golden haired sweetheart," murmured the driver of the rig as they turned and drove back to a narrow trail where the girl alighted. "My angel girl, my wife to be."

With a parting caress the golden haired one sped lightly home, entered the log farm house and sought the ice cold cubicle she called her room. She had lighted a small lamp and was surveying her rose and cream loveliness in a cracked mirror when her mother's voice called from the room below.

"That you, Lil?"

"Yes, Ma."

"Many out to meetin'?"

"Yes, the house was crowded."

"What made you so late?"

"There was a sort of row," the girl explained, telling half the truth. When the story was ended Mrs. May forgot her neuralgia in her enjoyment of a sensational story. Her daughter's late homecoming merged into a yawning pit which had abruptly swallowed the minister.

In the tiny room with its husk bed, its box-made table and white washed walls Lily sat before the cracked mirror and happily studied the pretty face that had miraculously attracted Steel and Hawley's bookkeeper. Presently with a sigh of satisfaction she undressed, slipped into her factory cotton night gown and into the icy bed. But Lily's sky blue eyes stared long at the moon yellowed window thinking of her miracle.

Later, Nordyke sat in an upper front room of the Agache boarding house before a paper covered table. Among the litter were letters, memorandum and a bank book. He examined the last with a speculative gaze then sat back and lighted a cigar. Into his mind swam the recent events of the evening and a vision of his late companion.

"The pretty fool! The ignorant mossback," he mused. "She's a handful of pale spring flowers. But it's you my queen of the night, that's worth the winning! I'll have you yet, you heathen priestess. When I've destroyed your property and am rid of that --."

Even in seclusion, Nordyke omitted the name of the one he hated and condemned to death.

XI

A District School Riot

During the second week of Mrs. Brett's school the Terrors and their sympathizers exhibited symptoms of malicious unrest. Small disturbances multiplied. Younger boys complained that they were targets for well-aimed missiles. Pupils emerging in orderly formation from their seats were tripped and send sprawling, but the perpetrators claimed the happenings to be unavoidable. Zoe Higbee aided, abetted and cheered on the insurgents. The old trinity of the world, the church and the devil applied to Mrs. Brett's school since District Number Four contained those for and against authority, and the opposition was generated by Satan himself.

Zoe Higbee joined the masculine toughs and declared war against Madeline. Ordinarily the girl would have groveled for recognition by a woman of Mrs. Brett's standing, but in school she desired boy worship. Lily May, Em Jobbin and their adherents, instead, gave the teacher a devotion to model themselves in her image as to dress and high coiled tresses. But when they tried to ape her refined, dignified and gentle deportment the result was simpering airs they thought fashionable. Lily May was too simple-hearted to appear other than she was – a loving, ignorant half child, half woman. She especially attached herself to Madeline and walked in her company to the shortcut to the May farm. Mrs. Brett returned Lily's devotion and spent extra hours preparing the girl for the spring examination. Because of this Lily formed the habit of spending Saturday afternoons in the Brett living room with her books. She was at the baize-covered table working out problems when Phil trapped his malodorous substitute for a coon.

Phil, with Sam shambling in the rear, was making the round of his traps when the Negro heard a startled yell.

"Hustle up, Sam," the boy's voice called. "Bruno's having a fit."

Sam quickly scrambled over intervening brush and saw the collie pup clawing at his smarting eyes with both paws and standing on his head in an agonized effort to rub his suffering nose. In a near trap was a black and white animal with a bushy tail which Phil had mercifully clubbed to death to his own undoing. He was in as much distress as Bruno and tightly clutched a handkerchief to his face.

"That's no coon," cried Phil. "He don't look like a coon, nor act like a coon, nor smell like a coon. He's awful!"

Sam, doubled in laughter, gasped out: "Skunk!"

"He's spoiled seven acres of woods," said Phil. "How so much smell got in that kitten beats me, and I'm in the same fix as Bruno. When I hit that cat I thought I'd strangle and the dog acted like he'd opened a box of ammonia. Guess I'll go to the house and change my clothes."

When the three hunters – Sam, Phil and Bruno – entered the kitchen Aunt Sally choked with horror and strangling scent. Madeline and Lily appeared on the scene demanding explanations.

"Land o' Goshen!" ejaculated Sally. "Git outen har. W'at dat boy been gittin' in?"

"Him ketched a new kin' er possum," said Sam, "an' he wants clean clo'es an' a wash."

"Go to the barn," Madeline directed, "and let Sam bring you a tub and clothes. You'll have to bury every stitch you've got on."

"And me with them," agreed Phil beyond the door. Gasping at the stench, Madeline brought Phil's clothing and dispatched hot water and home-made lye soap to his aid. It helped. But when Robert Floyd called that evening he found that the dominant odor still prevailed.

"You may break, you may shatter the vase if you will," he laughingly quoted, "but the attar of roses will cling to it still."

The incident of itself was bad enough but it furnished the Three Terrors material for their first open persecution of the hated city youth. His mental superiority, his gentlemanly appearance, his frank open manner and refinement were as a red rag to a ferocious bull. His ready surrender of a coveted seat slated him for a coward. They now agreed to make school so intolerable to him that he would leave, and they supposed him an easy conquest. Their opening attack was ridicule.

"Floyd's a heap big trapper," Quick sneered at intervals the following Monday. He had heard of Phil's skunk-clubbing episode.

"Traps coon," jeered Davitt.

"And plants his duds," shouted Sim.

"Say, Floyd, has them clothes sprouted yet?" grinned Davitt.

"Sure," sneered Rast Quick. "Don't he pick fresh ones every day? If you don't believe it look at him."

"Aw, quit your fooling," urged Em Jobbin. She had noticed a flame of color in their victim's sensitive face.

"Stop nothing," cried Davitt. "We ain't afraid of no girl-boy. He's just a sissy chap. Regular 'scholar'."

"At least I can to a triangle," he declared. Forthwith he knocked over Sim Parsons as if the gawky lad had been a nine-pin.

"That's the perpendicular," explained Phil. "Now for the base." He whirled on Davitt and landed a blow that enraged rather than injured the son of the camp pugilist. Sim had been routed so unexpectedly his allies had no time to interfere, now all three were on guard.

"I don't want none o' your help," shouted Davitt. "I kin lick him with one hand tied."

For a time it looked as if Bob Davitt had not boasted in vain. He was a gritty combatant. Then his slower wit opposed to Phil's gymnasium training placed him at the mercy of his slighter built adversary. In an unguarded moment Phil placed a blow that sent Davitt headlong to the ground where he lay slightly stunned.

Instantly Phil turned to Rast Quick, the lame member of the trio.

"Since you're not an isosceles," he told him, "I'll let you go. You know an isosceles is a triangle with equal legs." The vindictive thrust, utterly foreign to Phil's nature, hit the mark with the force of a shot. Rast turned livid with rage, but not a word escaped his tight shut lips. Next day Phil paid the price.

This tragic day had birth in a blinding snow fall that descended almost vertically through the still air. As the morning indicated no let up, Phil, as was his custom, started to school ahead of Madeline to make sure of a good fire in the box stove. According to district usage this duty of fire building belonged to the first comer, and Phil planned an early house warming.

Later, Madeline and Lily May, hurried through the big feathery flakes hurtling from a gray sky, and within sight of the school they became aware that the element of warmth was missing as no smoke rose from the chimney. Shivering children huddled about the door while within the stove in its shallow sand box was cold and ash-strewn. Phil was not there. Wondering at his absence Madeline gathered paper and kindling for a blaze and this with several dry blocks of wood soon created warmth and crackled cheerily up the flue. Billy Duff volunteered to bring in a further supply from the yard, and by nine o'clock the school assumed its usual order with each pupil in place excepting Phil. For a time Madeline was alarmed at the nonappearance of her boarder pupil. Then she remembered that Robert Floyd intended driving to Agache and suggested to Phil the advisability of accompanying him to purchase some needed clothing. Doubtless the lad met his father on the way to school and carried out this plan. Comforted by this explanation Madeline called the reading classes and listened to their halting phrases.

As the day advanced a spirit of outlawry filled the air. Feet dragged noisily along the floor. Books and slates were artfully dropped with startling crashes. An epidemic of thirst sent a procession of tip-toeing, shuffling, stomping children to the water pail near the door. Zoe Higbee ogled the Triangle of big boys with simpering smiles, and handed about clandestine notes. Gum was openly chewed despite the teacher's edict; impudent sneers passed at Madeline's back; a buzz of study and whispering set her already threadbare nerves on edge. Mob spirit was rife. The atmosphere was charged with incipient anarchy.

"Teacher, may I go out?" was a continual request from pupils who slammed the door. At noon the dining of forty children from dinner pails created an uproar peculiar to itself, and Madeline lacked an appetite for her own cold lunch. At one o'clock the reading classes straggled to place and Madeline weakly yielded to requests from Fifth Reader pupils for concert reading. Consequently Quick, Davitt, Zoe Higbee and others seized the opportunity to deafen ears with their loud rendering of "Old Rudiger."

Appalled at the uproar Madeline dismissed the blatant readers and called the Fourth. This class was fated to relate the ear-splitting tragedy of Marco Bozzaris. Of course, the nervous tension in the air predisposed Billy Duff to helpless, spasmodic laughter. So when Sim Parson attempted to declaim the Turk's dream Billy exploded. Sim's idea of the text was hazy but his mind was impressed with a parrot like memory of the alluring meter. Without pause or inflection he dragged through the lines:

"At midnight in – his – guarded – tent – the – Turk – lay – dreaming – of – the – hour – when – grease-er-knee- when – grease-er-knee –"

Here memory failed and Billy laughed himself into spasms. As a matter of urgent necessity Madeline was forced to terminate Sim' lubricating idea and desert Marco Bozzaris to die unaided.

As afternoon wore on the tumult deepened. Lily May cast indignant glances at the lawbreakers without effect. No one but a pioneer teacher can understand the extent of this school riot. Requests were unheeded, commands were openly disobeyed. Rast Quick snatched Billy Duff's slate and let the whole smash in fragments on the floor.

"That's an outrage," Madeline told him.

The lame tough began to mumble that it was an accident when Zoe Higbee hastily confirmed his lying statement.

"He didn't mean to," she affirmed impudently. "I seen the hull of it, and Rast just –."

"Hold your tongue," sharply ordered the exasperated teacher. Her southern temper was ablaze.

"Hold nothin'," flared Zoe. "I don't have to shut my mouth for a nigger! Let me tell you that."

For a moment the room stilled to a dead silence then rose to an uproar at the insult. If Madeline had attempted – as the school expected – to mete out punishment havoc would have ensued with the Terrors protecting Zoe in a bitter fight. Instead Madeline faced the insurrectionists with a face like death and black eyes blazing. Her poise was regal as her burning gaze searched each countenance. Then clarion clear, thrilling with anger and despair, vibrating with power, rising to musical volume, holding the rebels spellbound, shaming them, mastering them, Madeline sang the wielding hymn:

"Master, the tempest is raging,
The billows are tossing high:
My sky is o'ershadowed with darkness,
No shelter or help is nigh."

Came the significant chorus in notes low as the first muttering of a storm and rising in fearful crescendo until the otherwise silent room rang with the prophesy:

"Whether the wrath of the storm-tossed sea
Or demons, or men, or whatever they be,
They all shall sweetly obey my will,
Peace be still, peace be still.
They all shall sweetly obey my will,
Peace, peace, be still."

When the agonized song prayer ended Madeline knew she had conquered. The compelling song had given the renegaded a vision beyond their narrow horizon. As the splendid voice enveloped the evil doers in pulsing, heaven-storming melody Zoe Higbee and the Terrors faded into a dim perspective and their importance dwindled to nothing at all. The school stared at the beautiful singer and listened to her inspired song forgetting the rebels. Without a word concerning the happening Madeline resumed classes. The room remained unnaturally still. Finally came the welcome closing hour and the teacher was alone with bare walls, empty benches and her bitter memory. She had donned wraps and overshoes and was ready to step into the white storm when the door opened and framed the stalwart form of Robert Floyd.

"This is such a beastly storm," said the manager, "that I decided to give you and Phil a ride home."

"What!" cried Madeline. "Isn't Phil with you?"

"No," said the mystified manager.

"Then," said Madeline, white to the lips, "God protect him! He's been gone since morning. What can it mean?"

XII

The Search for Phil

At the camp belated teamsters straggled to a late supper; others circled the four sided fireplace and related their never failing stories of former hard winters. Tobacco smoke wrapped them in a blue haze like distant mountain tops in autumn. Mike Munshaw, six foot in his socks, brawny, agile and enduring as oak, sat with his great shoulders braced against a lower bunk, his arms embracing a knee and his short clay pipe adding to the thickened atmosphere. His bronzed visage wore an expression of tranquil peace and his manner was the sober, quiet, undemonstrative attitude of the typical lumberjack. He was coarse, but his coarseness was that of the towering pine. He partook of the calm majesty of the unbroken forest; his thoughts were of timber – cutting, rafting, turning to lumber.

"By Jing' the Company's spreading big this winter," shrilled Bill Watson as he seated himself by the fire after a late supper.

"Ya," agreed Anderson. "I tank da firm bane awful much to do by spring."

"If the Company ain't edging over on the Blair tract," opined Chet Brooks, "I'm a sucker."

"You'll be something else if you don't look out," warned Dan Hilliker with a nudge in the speaker's ribs. "You'll be out of a job."

Mann, who appeared at the moment after copying his tally sheets, glanced at Stimson as Chet voiced his suspicion. The bush-monkey's ferret face assumed an expression of alert watchfulness. His small eyes reminded the scaler of a cat at a mouse hole. Next he studied Brinkley who was reading by a lamp on a barrel-head.

"I wonder if our church-going boss suspects his firm of crooked work," pondered the tallier. But the thought perished. Jovial, big hearted Brinkley would never countenance a shady deal. Floyd, the new manager, must also be ignorant of the timber limits. But suddenly he recalled an image of Pete Markham, the surveyor, who had staked out the boundary. The man was long bodied with a small head and receding chin. Instinctively Mann felt repulsion for the surveyor at their chance meeting in Agache. Now he wondered if the agreeable Mr. Markham had been bribed to trickery. He decided at the first opportunity to use his knowledge of the surveying art to test that gentlemen's accuracy. Then he thought of Brett and also cleared the former manager of guilty knowledge. Whatever motive sent Brett from the spot it was not connivance at treachery. The whole matter was baffling, so for the time he dismissed it and lifted Tam O'Shanter to his knee for a frolic as the outer door burst open and admitted Sam from the Brett household.

"Marse Floyd tole me git men ter hunt fo' dat chile, Phil," he gasped. "He's done been lost sence morning. An' his paw say yo' hatter come quick or de pore boy boun' ter freeze."

Mann and Brinkley were at Sam's side asking questions before the last words left his quivering lips. When the facts were learned Brinkley called for volunteer searchers.

"I'm with you," shouted many voices. Men began to pull on discarded socks and wet shoe packs. In a few minutes most of the camp marched toward the Brett clearing which was to be a starting point for a thorough hunt.

"This is a devil of a night for the job," Rube Kinney remarked to the man ahead of him. "Snow'll cover tracks level, or even a body," he added in a lower key.

At the Brett farm they found Jud Coon in rag-dangling garments who was efficiently employed in preparing pitch-pine torches.

"Grab one apiece, boys," he greeted them in his high falsetto, "and light 'em at that bonfire. We're going to comb the woods where the kid set traps."

Robert Floyd, believing his son was perishing in the woods, left Jud in charge of the lighting and set out alone. He knew Brinkley would organize the searching party as he promptly did.

"Munshaw, you and Hilliker take the center and far end of the line while the boys deploy along the road twenty feet apart. Mann and I will manage this end. When everything's ready we move south. Understand?"

"Yes," shouted a chorus.

"Call the lad's name every five rods and listen for an answer."

"We will."

"And examine every spot where a body might be covered."

Silence greeted this tragic command as the procession divided into points of flaring red that grimly punctuated the snow filled darkness. Presently the center men passed Floyd whose face was stern with repressed anxiety, his eyes set in black hollows, his voice as he thanked the searchers, was hoarse with misery.

"Surely," he said when he neared Mann, "Phil wouldn't leave the vicinity of his traps."

"We don't know what happened," the scaler told him. "But we'll find him. The men will move along and swing back. They can't miss."

The forest was lighted by a strange radiance and echoed with weird calls as many torch bearers moved slowly through clogging snow and impeding brush. Night birds fluttered in bewilderment as searchers inspected each mound of white, each snow-imbedded tree, each snow-capped stump. At the end of a mile Hilliker formed the men in a new swath that swept back to the main highway. And again they met Floyd and sifted by.

"Wouldn't we cover more ground if the men scattered?" he asked Brinkley in a voice dull with despair.

"No," said the foreman. "Instead of slow certainty we'd be trusting to luck."

Three times the blazing flambeaux, often replaced or relighted, swept a square mile of forest while the bearers shouted the monotonous cry of "Phil! Oh, Phil!"

Suddenly, within a hundred feet of the blazed trail, Hod Elwin let loose a cry that surpassed his best efforts at a county dance.

"Here's the lad," he yelled, "fast in a bear trap!"

The joyful news traveled along the line of hunters with the speed of an electric current and immediately lights began to converge until a circle of rugged faces stared at what Hod lifted from its bed of snow by a fallen log. One of the unconscious boy's feet was clamped in the black jaws of a powerful steel trap while a chain circled the log to which it was locked.

"Yon's the boy all right," Munshaw said in the hushed tone of one who fears the worst.

"He's not dead," decided Brinkley who was making a hasty examination. "The worst is the trapped foot. That may be frozen."

"Here's a fox trap just beyond," discovered Watson. "The animal in it is frozen stiff. Happened to hit it with my foot."

Two men pried apart the relentless jaws of the bear trap and released Phil's foot just as Mann came up with Floyd. The latter held his son in his arms while Hilliker busied himself with the foot that had been so many hours in a vice-like grip. The boy's heavy boot and thick wool sock had prevented ligaments being torn, but blood had ceased to circulate. Being familiar with every degree of frost bite the big lumberjack knew there was a chance to save the frozen member. With handsfull of snow he rubbed the bare foot while Jim Sprik offered a flash of spirits he had not had time to imbibe.

"Not now, Jim," Hilliker refused. "If the lad comes to while blood tried to get back in his foot he'd be crazy with pain."

"Hadn't we better take him home?" asked Floyd, his face white with anxiety.

"Not till the frost is rubbed out," insisted Hilliker. "If warm air gets to him he'd lose his foot. Have patience, Mr. Floyd. See! The muscles are limbering up and the skin's getting red. Now take Jim's likker and bathe his face and hands."

As Floyd removed Phil's thick mittens to carry out Hilliker's order Phil opened his eyes and a weak voice said, "That wasn't my trap, Dad. I never set it, but it got me. Now I want to go home."

"Most anybody'd want to go home after a day in a bear pincher," agreed Brinkley.

"It wasn't a bear trap. It was a Phil trap," came unexpectedly from the suffering youth. "It was set for me and pad-locked so I couldn't escape. I walked into it with my fox over there as bait."

"Who trapped you, Phil?" asked his father, but Phil was silent. And again he lost consciousness as lumberjacks lifted him to an improvised stretcher. The pain of his trapped foot was beyond endurance and merciful oblivion intervened in his favor.

Before going the manager turned to the forms outlined against the torch-lighted forest.

"Jim has orders to serve you hot coffee," he told them. "I know you are tired and wet from the tramp and were tired and wet from the day's work. You have been true friends. You saved my boy." His voice choked. "I won't forget."

At the Brett cottage they found Madeline waiting in an agony of apprehension.

"He's only in a swoon," Floyd hastened to assure her, then briefly told all he knew.

"Put him on the couch," she directed. "I'll watch while you all eat lunch. Sally has it ready." Hilliker and Munshaw considered Sally's coffee and rolls with cake and doughnuts ample reward for their service. It was a memorable meal shared by the manager and scaler who soon rejoined the injured boy and were amazed to see him sitting up before a tray Sally had provided according to her idea of a famished boy's appetite. Madeline had ministered successfully to her favorite's aching extremity and watched with shining eyes while he ate Sally's dainties.

"What? Up and at it!" his father exclaimed. Once more his blue eyes laughed and his lips smiled. "You won't even be crippled," he gloated. "You'll walk on both feet."

"I didn't get very cold," Phil explained. "The snow covered me and my clothes were an Arctic outfit. Besides, there's no zero weather with big snowflakes. You see I was lucky."

"I see you are here. That's enough for me – now," said his grateful parent.

When Mann, after an hour's delay, followed the big lumberjacks to camp he had the curious sensation of being under surveillance. The impression seemed absurd, yet he regretted not accompanying the stretcher bearers. His hour with Floyd had been spent in a discussion of Phil's recent plight and the possible perpetrators of the crime.

Neither the two men nor Madeline doubted that the Triangle was responsible for the outrage, yet proof was lacking. Although bear traps were not plentiful in the settlement they were difficult to identify. Moreover the trap might have been stolen from an innocent individual. But the fiendish plot was perfect in detail even to luring the victim into the hidden steel by means of a fox in his own trap. Bob Stray had discovered that the animal had been twice a captive. Its death had occurred hours before Phil discovered its life-like shape in a trap he had set far from his usual beat.

With nothing decided Mann had started for camp thinking to visit the Blair skidways before turning in. He strode along haunted by an unaccountable sense of danger, and suddenly he heard behind him the snapping of a dead twig. Instantly he stepped back of a huge hemlock. Just in time. The stillness of night was shattered by the report of a gun. It sounded close in the rear but when the scaler rushed to seize the assassin no one was there. Evidently the thug lacked nerve for a second attack. Suspicion of the would- be murderer's identity sent Mann racing to camp that he might verify his conclusion.

Within the bunk house a few still lingered by the fire. Watson was thrusting his curly head into his cloth cap before retiring, and had one foot on the lower bunk ready to mount.

"What you gitting into your cap for?" demanded Dan Bateman as he amazedly eyed Watson's night arrangement. "'Tain't time to hitch the team. 'Tain't morning."

"I know 'tain't morning," said Watson. "But I aim to git up without pulling my hair out. Last night it froze to the bunk, by Jing. Had to cut myself loose. Thought I'd start in right and save trouble."

Mann, entering, examined a certain bunk at the end of the room. It was Stimson's bed and it was empty. Nor was the bush-monkey by the fireplace.

"Where's Stimson?" the scaler asked Brinkley.

"Gone to Agache," the boss told him. "He'll be back by morning."

"Then he lingered by the way," thought the tallier, and realized that he had missed death by a narrow margin.

XIII

The Quilting Bee

School during the remaining three days of that week was an era of absolute peace. The Triangle furtively eyed the teacher but appeared intent on their lessons. Zoe Higbee expected sensational retribution would overtake all who had offended Madeline but the teacher turned her back squarely on the insurgents and calmly conducted her classes. Phil, of course, remained at home to heal his swollen foot but he studied the lessons given out in school and recited to Madeline in the evening. Meanwhile the settlement discussed his unpleasant experience and it was the chief topic during a quilting bee at the Groot farm house besides other gossip of breathless interest.

"Sarah told me," observed Mrs. Coon from her corner of the album-pattern quilt, "that our teacher sang like an angel the day them boys acted up. Said she looked sort of like a white coal of fire an' that her black eyes burnt into everybody when she sang about demons. My, it was awful."

"She had no business telling Zoe to shut her mouth," declared Mrs. Higbee, biting off a thread viciously and glancing about with the bold gaze of her impudent daughter.

Mrs. Groot chalked a line on the quilt and remarked with the sly, indulgent laugh that prefaced devilish innuendo, "Mrs. Brett ought not get mad when folks mentions her relatives," she hinted.

"Specially if they has nigger blood in them," said Sim's mother, coming out in the open. "Proves she's part nigger or she wouldn't get riled."

"Mrs. Brett's at least octoroon," stated Mrs. Roth to whom nothing was sacred. Her Roman nose and keen gray eyes indicated native intelligence. "That queer complexion of hers – olive they call it in story books – means negro blood. She'd never keep them two darkeys living on her earnings unless they was relatives, and people say she calls 'em aunt and uncle."

"So do folks call you aunt," defended Mrs. Coon. "Most everybody calls you Aunt Belinda, but that don't make it do."

"You mind what I say," continued Mrs. Roth, ignoring the peace-maker. "Sooner or later you'll find Brett left his wife for more reasons than her flirting with the scaler." Her tone lowered to a confidential pitch. "You'll find he left her on account of that nigger blood."

Several women gasped in horror but Mrs. Higbee added something more sensational.

"I don't notice," said she, "that Mrs. Brett cares about Brett's going, or the scaler leaving her for that India Blair. Fact is she's set a trap for the new manager that'll hold longer than the one that catched the boy. Her taking that lad to board shows which way the wind blows. She's bound to be the wife of another manager. You'll see!"

"Maybe," agreed Mrs. Roth, "but the scaler can run after India Blair till he's black in the face as the Brett niggers and it won't do him no good. Her cap's set for Nordyke and she ain't going to favor no man that comes from Lord-knows-where. She'd be a fool."

Mrs. Groot's announcement of lunch transferred the ladies from the quilt to the crowded table with its three kinds of preserves, its four sorts of cake, its biscuits and boiled ham. And the demolition of food ended the onslaught on innocent neighbors.

That same Saturday afternoon Mrs. Swisher knocked sharply at the Brett kitchen door, closed it with a half slam and settled in the customary low rocker. She was out to interview the hero of a torch-light search and found him occupying an arm chair in the cook's freshly scrubbed domain.

"How on earth did you keep from freezing?" she demanded after hearing Phil relate the particulars of his adventure.

"Flapped my arms," he explained. "Flapped my arms by count – one, two, three. And I moved my loose foot and slapped the trapped one as long as I knew anything to keep up circulation."

"Humph," said Mrs. Swisher. "Got a dose of your own dope. What do you think of trapping after feeling it?"

"It's the Spanish inquisition applied to animals," cried Phil "I'll never set another trap. Never again, Mrs. Swisher."

"Who ketched you?" inquired the caller.

"I don't know," hedged Phil. "Anyway, they won't get me again."

Mrs. Swisher turned to Madeline who was peeling apples for Sally's pies.

"I hears you sung them young devils into a fit," she said with a burst of laughter. "Sung 'em into the first decency that ever struck 'em. And now I wish you'd go over to Bender's and sing them poker fiends into spasms. They played till broad daylight Sunday morning. Mis' Jobbin told me that Jobbin said Nordyke went home with two hundred dollars of the fools' cash, and he'd got more for Bender getting the rest outen them for likker. To my notion he's a better man than Nordyke since he gives 'em a dose of poison for their money."

"Why is it better for Bender to poison them than for the bookkeeper to steal from them?" inquired Madeline.

"Because doped whiskey kills 'em off," jerked out the critic. "Nordyke he lets 'em live and picks 'em periodic."

"Rudder a heap hab 'em 'en turkeys," remarked Aunt Sally. Catching the last phrase as she emerged from the pantry. "Turkeys are jus' natural born scalawags. One lone turkey hen c'n think up more devilment than a hull yard full o' poetry. There was that Jenny hen -." Sally descanted on turkey depravity until Mrs. Swisher rose to go.

"Spose I'll see all of you to meeting," she smiled. "Hope the elder won't drop though the floor. It's upsettn' to have the preacher interrupted thataway. Coon, he's nailed enough boards under and over them planks to keep up an elephant. He don't calculate to lose no more preachers, not Coon."

Laughing heartily the energetic caller said good-bye, flounced out with the abruptness David Johnathan went through the floor and was on her fleet-footed way.

That Saturday Mann as usual turned in his reports to the Company's bookkeeper and to Blair at Blair's mill, but he stopped at the latter place on his way back and directed his driver, Jules Deveraux, to go to camp alone.

He found India Blair in her office jotting down the week's mill accounts and her handsome face was radiant.

"See that!" said she, pointing at a balance sheet. "We've cleared over a hundred dollars this week above cutting, hauling, wages for the mill crew, incidentals and supplies for the boarding house. It's the first gain in months."

"There won't be any more spiked logs," promised Mann as he seated himself opposite India by a red-shaded lamp that tinted their faces and scattered papers with a rosy glow. "And your profits will soon reduce your debt to a cipher.

"Now for my tally," he said, producing his book. "I'll read the numbers and you take them down. Skidway No. One," he commenced, "twenty seven twelve foot logs, entire scale: four thousand, eight hundred forty two."

"A poor lot," commented India. "All right. Go on."

"Skidway No. Two, twenty four sixteen foot pine logs. Entire scale: seven thousand, two hundred and eighty."

"Yes," said India with a pencil poised for a new item. Her manner was practical and business like as they worked until the task ended. Then they discussed the sensational happening of the week. But India was observing the play of expression on the scaler's countenance while Mann studied the bewitching face opposite and finally voiced the warning that was ever in his mind.

"Don't drive about unattended," he begged of her. "It is dangerous. It is folly. Have someone with you. Your mother -."

"Is an invalid," India cut in with curious eyes on his face.

"Then take one of the men - Matt Crane or Shawnoga."

"Impossible," cried the amazed mill owner. She flamed with anger. Could this man of mystery not understand? Was he ignorant of settlement custom?

For a moment Mann was tempted to relate the attempt of his life as what might happen to Blair, but he refrained. It would add to her anxiety about himself.

"Your driving alone is madness," he said sharply.

"Nonsense," flared India. "My enemies may wreck the mill but they won't attack a woman. I'm safe at any hour of the day or night."

"Your enemies are desperate scoundrels," said Mann. "There's something back of this neither you or I can grasp. I won't have you go blindly into danger. After this I'll see that you arrive safely home."

"Just how?" demanded India, eyes half closed but hard and bright.

"By guarding you myself," he told her.

India burst into forgiving laughter. Mann's singleness of purpose, his blindness, his masculine innocence were attractions that endeared him to her a thousand fold. But she wanted him to read deeper and learn the truth – that she adored him.

He parted from the girl lumberjack with a quiet good-night and a lift of the hat, but dared not touch her hand. He lacked the courage for intimate contact. In the lower living room India happily mused of the man who had pledged himself to act as her body guard, and she rejoiced. Instead of his usual aloofness he would be at her side and she decided the necessity should be frequent.

But had India known of the horse without bells by the skidway, of Stimson's cunning, of the shot in the dark and Mann's mounting suspicions she might have been less confident in her immunity from harm, and would have agonized over the scaler's return to camp which he reached without incident and was astonished to find Floyd lingering among roughnecks at the fireside. The men were ominously silent. There was no Saturday night story telling. Floyd, seeing the scaler appear, motioned him to a seat at his side.

"We've had a bad accident," he told Mann. "The binding chain on Bob Davitt's load snapped in two, and the logs caught him before he could jump clear. I guess he's done for. His right leg is crushed and he's spitting blood from a jammed chest. He may live till morning."

"Where is he?" asked Mann.

"We took him home. It happened on his last load – last load sure enough, poor chap. Hilliker went ahead to prepare his wife for the shock, but she's half crazed and utterly useless. Neighbors did what they could and young Bob hustled off after Mrs. Brett."

"And a doctor?" added the scaler. "Mrs. Brett ought not be alone if Davitt's dying."

"Tom Borden rushed after a doctor with my team," the manager assured him. But it's useless. Davitt won't live till Tom reaches Hickory Vale."

"You're going back?" It was a question.

"Yes," said Floyd. "At ten I'm to take Mrs. Brett home. I wish you'd accompany me and see if there's anything to be looked after."

Mann readily consented, and at the hour named the two neared Davitt's cabin where a kerosene light yellowed small paned windows that blinked tearfully as if aware of the tragedy in the low-raftered room. On an improvised bed lay Bat Davitt and by his side watching every labored breath, sat Madeline. Her own countenance resembled Davitt's in ghastly pallor, but her attitude was alert and her dark eyes intent upon her almost dying patient.

At an elevated oven cook stove sat two women – Mrs. Jobbin and Mrs. May. Near them with his face covered by roughened hands was Bob, the main stay of the three Terrors. Gone was his dare devil nonchalance. He was stricken dumb by this unbelievable calamity to his household. None knew better than he that Brinkley and Jim Sprik patiently waited for the moment when their services would be required to dress the dead.

"Where is Bat's wife?" Floyd asked Brinkley in a whisper.

The foreman motioned toward a rude, open stair.

"Sleeping under the influence of an opiate. She carried on so fierce Mrs. Brett had to get her out of the way."

"And the children?"

"Over at Jud Coon's, except Bob."

Floyd stepped to Madeline and touched her shoulder.

"I'm here to take you home," he reminded her.

"I'm not going," she told him softly. "My place is here for I believe this man can be saved. His open air work and giant's constitution are in his favor. Have Sally pack me some loose gowns, slippers and suitable food. And make some arrangements for the Davitts to board temporarily with Jud Coon. We must eliminate the sound and odor of preparing meals. If everything goes right we may save both life and limb."

"This is madness," remonstrated Floyd. "Remember the school, and your other cares."

"There shall be no school, no care but this until I'm relieved by a physician and my conscience."

"If that's your last word," conceded Floyd, "we'll at least tend to your comfort."

He started at once for the Brett farm to do her bidding and met Jud Coon and Abe Jobbin going to the house of mourning for the death watch. Mann accompanied the manager to camp, but his errand was to make doubly sure that Stimson kept his word with regard to stopping over Sunday in Agache.

By the time Floyd returned to Davitt's with the articles Madeline required dawn was bleaching the east, and the high floating crescent of new moon had paled to a blur. At the Davitt gate stood a jaded team whose haggard driver was just alighting.

"I couldn't fetch no doctor," stated Tom Bordon wearily. "He was over toward the bay – smallpox in the east camps. Anyhow I knew it wan't no use bringing no doc to a dead man."

XIV

Making Maple Sugar

During the following two weeks Madeline Brett battled valiantly with death while the entire settlement breathlessly watched the result. Callers saw Bat Davitt, the local pugilist and all around tough, lying helplessly on a snow white pillow of his nurse's furnishing while his eyes observed Madeline with a puzzled stare. Mrs. Davitt, gaunt, nervous and incapable, obeyed the self-appointed doctor's least suggestion while Bob, the Terror, rendered dog-like fidelity and whole hearted devotion to the teacher he once despised.

At the end of the first week Mrs. Brett made two illuminating discoveries concerning Bob. First she became aware that Mrs. Davitt was not his own mother, and second his stepmother was far from being congenial. It was not long before Bob made a voluntary confession that he had aided in trapping Phil. He made no defense, and was ready to pay the penalty of his crime. Madeline realized that he suffered acutely from shame and regret. She was unintentionally heaping coals of fire that burned away his coarseness and revealed generous impulses. When she made known to Floyd the facts Bob had blurted out she asked that the offender be left to her mercy.

"Deal with him – and the others – as you think best," permitted the manager. "If you can save both father and son you've surely earned the right to act as judge and jury."

So Madeline in the capacity of judge and jury deferred action while she continued her ministrations to her rallying patient. Bat Davitt's iron physique triumphed, but there remained weeks of bitter endurance while the compound fracture knitted and healed into a sound limb, and all this time Madeline not only taught school but daily called at the Davitt's to examine the bandages and splints, care for the patient's general health and quell his profane impatience.

School was a surprise. The chinked walls, the deal benches, the bare windows, the water pail by the door and the square stove in its shallow box of sand welcomed her like home while the children greeted their teacher with shy delight. Yet, Madeline, as she rang the last bell, sat observant and apprehensive until the older pupils sifted into place, Zoe Higbee, head in air and ready for trouble, preempted a rear seat; but to Zoe's – and Madeline's astonishment – the opposite seat, usually occupied by the Terrors, was taken by Dan Jobbin. Zoe had been deserted by her masculine aids to mischief. Then to the school's gaping amazement Phil and Bob Davitt tossed their books on the same desk and shared a seat. Madeline rejoiced. These two boys shared her devotion and she was overwhelmingly glad they had buried the hatchet – or bear trap – and become pals. It ended any idea of prosecuting the trappers, and peace and sanity descended upon the school in District Number Four.

Before long the deep snow softened by day but froze to granite firmness by night. Bare stretches of black earth appeared in highways and fields. It became necessary for Steel and Hawley's night gangs to sprinkle logging roads with a water cart that they might freeze into condition for the next day's haul. Then April was ushered in by a salvo of heaven's artillery, and the same triumphant salute marked the last day of the settlement school.

After that Phil, assisted by Sam, joined the universal sugar making. In every settler's bush wooden troughs caught the sweet sap of maple trees and from many kettles rose sweet incense. Sally watched her brightly scoured tins being devoted to the saccharine cause with lively protests; but Sam ignored his wife's grumbling since, like old drugs, it had lost its disturbing power.

Each morning Phil presided over the iron kettle of violently boiling sap while Sam gathered the overflow that frosty nights and sunny days sent into the various pails, tubs, crocks and pans abstracted from Sally's precincts. Frequently the thin syrup threatened to boil over but a dipper of fresh sap cooled its ardor or a pork rind kept down the volcanic sweet. As Phil cut brush one morning to stoke his fire Jud Coon stopped on his way to Agache.

"Hello," he genially greeted the sap-boiler. "Thought I'd see how you was getting on with sugaring."

"We've got it to burn," cried Phil.

"Yes, sir; sap's running wild," commented Mr. Coon. "We filled a tub with soft an' calculate to sugar off two hundred weight of hard 'fore sap quit. Soft is what the Injuns sell in birch-bark baskets. You ought-a see 'em make it. Sure's I'm born every kettle has a muskrat tied to the handle by his tail; when the syrup rairs up it gits grease outen the varmint's snout and settles back like it wants to git away."

Having disclosed this unsavory information Mr. Coon laughed uproariously, returned to his dozing mare, and proceeded to town.

"We uns hatter boil all night," announced Sam, arriving with pails of sap pendent from his neck-yoke. "Dat bush is jes' spilling ober."

Consequently that night and many others found a circle of forest brilliant with leaping flames. Everywhere settlers duplicated this saccharine vigil and sugaring off parties were held wherever ascended the odorous syrup-laden steam. Madeline summoned India Blair to join them Saturday night when Floyd and Mann assisted at the orgies. And India, arriving early, encountered Sally with a double handful of fresh laid eggs.

"Dam fool critters didn't git 'em," she gloated in an extraordinary form of greeting.

"What? The eggs?" laughed India.

"Yes'm" Sally explained. "Dem pesky hens done et their heads off, an' now dey want to lay roun' an' eat dere eggs. Dey do a good act den bust it open. Yes'm, poetry is awful human."

"How did you come?" cried Madeline in astonishment, not seeing Billy-boy.

"Walked," confessed India. "It's a delight to tread bare spots. As for the rivulets I wanted to sail boats on them."

"I'll keep you over night," planned Madeline. "And tomorrow. You know there's church at the school house. We'll all go."

They were in the bush when Floyd and Mann joined them. Phil's generous fire burned a flickering circle from the velvet night and nearby sap-spouts dripped slowly falling rubies into tinkling pails while Sally bent over a pan of thickly bubbling sweet.

"It's almost ready for wax," proclaimed India. Each absorbed face glowed in the firelight. Drifting steam enveloped the group like a filmy veil and Phil's last contribution to the coals sent up a shower of sparks.

"You're posing," Floyd accused them.

"What! You here?" Mann cried, seeing India. His eyes glowed with delight, but his voice had an edge remembering his warning.

"Why not?" defied the girl lumberjack. "I'm here and I walked." She laughed outright at his look of dismay.

"You're mad," he accused her, seating himself of the log at her side. "You're foolhardy."

"When I become a prisoner," declared India, "I'll be my own keeper."

Mann was thoughtfully gazing at the leaping flame, but what he saw was a skulking form near that very spot and what he heard was the crash of a shot in a cowardly attempt on his life.

"I believe," he said finally, "that the next move will be something original, different. These thugs are inventive. They won't repeat."

"What do you mean?" asked India, defiance gone.

"There will be no more spikes in the logs. The next attempt to stop payment on your mortgage will be something unforeseen."

Their discussion was interrupted by Madeline and Sally who brought them helpings of hot syrup boiled to a point where it would quickly stir to soft sugar or turn to wax. Floyd and Phil supplied snow from shaded hollows for wax-making. And Bruno remained by Sam to share his syrup spread on snow which was warranted to clog the pup's teeth until clawing paws relieved his pleasant misery.

When the coals were banked for the night and the party started to the Brett farm house Floyd and Phil walked ahead of Sam's lantern while Madeline and Sally followed. But India, by feminine wiles inconsistent to a hard headed mill owner, managed to keep the scaler at the rear. Once she would have fallen but her escort intervened a strong arm and also firmly clasped the hand she extended for help. Thus with her warm fingers in his protecting palm the unavowed lovers passed slowly over patches of snow, the leafy arcades of forest and the fields that led to the lamp lighted cottage.

"When do you go home?" Mann questioned as they paused at the Brett door before parting."

"Right after church tomorrow," India told him, wondering what he would decide.

"Then I'll be on hand to see you don't get a shot on the back," he said grimly. "We'll discount the risk."

Floyd, bearing a lantern, joined them. Both men bade India good night, secured the manager's team, and departed to their separate lodgings.

"I don't understand him," mused India as she stood brushing her thick, dark hair before the glass in Madeline's guest room. "He loves me; he trembles at my touch; he is in terror at the chance of my being in peril; his eyes betray his secret yet he treats me exactly as he does Robert Floyd. He accords to me the courtesy due a woman and the friendship he'd give a man. I won't stand for it. I'll have love – and the expression of it. There's no reason we shouldn't wed. He's only a scaler and I'm only a mill owner swamped with debt. We're both lumberjacks. Common sense points to a union between us. He <u>shall</u> make love to me. It's my human right. Before high heaven it's a woman's just due."

Next evening the school house was crowded to the door. A mild night that hinted of imminent green in woods and fields brought out both regular and irregular goers. To Madeline the settlers showed a new deference. She had become a local idol by sheer will and kindness of heart. The gossips of the memorable quilting bee glanced at one another uneasily hoping their spiteful remarks were forgotten. Each one listened eagerly as the teacher's glorious voice rose unfaltering in the evening hymn and reminded the congregation of the day she had sung into submission a childish revolt. Observant eyes noted that Mrs. Davitt shared a triple bench with Mrs. Brett and India Blair. Stragglers also found a fertile topic for discussion in the fact that Steel and Hawley's tally man had purchased a black driving horse, and that when he left the school house grounds India Blair was seated at his side.

During the ride lakeward through the moonless forest the tallier's manner toward India was distinctly that of a business friend. He determined that, equally as he guarded her from assassin, he would also guard her from himself.

"I'm an unspeakable cad," he thought, "to worship this girl when there's no hope – and much danger. I may be a fool to play with fire, but I'm not a villain enough to make love to a woman I can never marry."

When he assisted India to alight at her gate the girl's warm breath swept his cheek, her supple form was within his arms. For a moment he longed wildly to crush her to his heart, to possess himself of her full red lips. Two souls hungered for each other. But the two vigorous natures, pulsing with vitality were separated as by bars of steel. The man's high standard of action, the woman's heritage of custom built between them as impassible barrier.

Mrs. Blair looked placidly up from her book as India entered the downstairs living room. By the light of the reading lamp she noticed her daughter's cheeks were hotly flushed, the dark eyes aflame; yet the girl appeared like one groping in the dark. She was trying to fathom motives beyond her understanding, to solve a mystery.

"Am I, a woman lumberjack, not good enough for this man?" she asked herself. Then her head flung up and her eyes flashed.

"Yes," she judged. "Before God and man I am his equal. No one living may disdain a Blair."

XV

What Bob Stray Found

Thaw winds roared through bare tree tops, earth-soiled snow disappeared under April showers until only ragged heaps lay in hollows or on shaded hill sides, and Muskrat Lake boomed and thundered in its ice-breaking agony. At Slabtown on the west shore the Company's great mill was a scene of activity as men hastened preparations for the season's cut. At the slab-built pier a tug named Indian Queen was being refitted to tow rafts of logs to the empty boom when waves danced where groaning ice promised a speedy break-up. Northward a wooden tram track connected the mill with the Company's dock on Lake Michigan and moved the season's lumber on horse drawn cars.

As yet Long Jim's dinner horn summoned only a dozen of the former camp crew to the mill boarding house. Lumberjacks waited the movement of ice in the lake before a full crew would be needed. A few remained in the winter camp trucking in the remaining logs of the largest cut ever piled on the

Muskrat rollways. And Bob Stray used his enforced vacation for an interval of sport.

One day, armed with a rifle, the lad with the forgotten past started forth in quest of deer. His choice of direction was back of camp, and by chance he trod almost the same course taken by Mann the Sunday he became lost. For an hour Bob circled in and out among endless hills and valleys searching game not then protected by closed seasons. Because the mellow spring air induced a feeling of lassitude he cared little for the success of his mission. In was a joy to idle on and on over leaf-covered ground in the friendly solitude. Frequently he made detours to avoid lingering snow cupped in hollows. Whether his line of travel was direct or devious didn't matter. It was guide enough to know that the rending ice of Muskrat Lake roared in the distance.

A darting woodcock with crimson crest passed him like a spurt of flame. Near and far the long drawn notes of the phoebe drifted through the forest like liquid melody. Several times the dull spotted gray of a partridge scuttled in the underbrush, and the heaven blue plumage of jays appeared in the open. Toward evening the bird sounds muted and storm clouds hastened twilight. A rabbit dashed by him followed by a flash of dull red and Bob knew a deer had sped into the deeper forest. Although his gun lay across his shoulder he was too astonished at the swift appearance of the game he sought to take aim. The deer was gone like a glint of lightening and he stood by a hemlock staring.

Next instant the hunter was amazed to see the distant form of a man bending over the graying snow in a hollow. The day had grown too dark from clouds and coming night to note the man's identity but he wore the customary mackinaw, and he wielded some tools as if in the act of burying treasure.

"One of the cattle thieves," decided Bob, and flattened himself behind his shelter. A cattle rustler was not a person to be encountered especially while concealing something he wished to hide. Presently the lone thief seemed to be satisfied with his task and slipped westward like a shadow.

"I'm going to see what he hid," decided Bob. "It won't take long. Probably a wad of shang."

Taking heed that the owner of the treasure trove had not changed his mind about leaving, Bob crept among tree trunks to the spot. Then with the sharp section of a broken limb he probed and threw back loosened earth. At last his hand came in contact with a substance that he grasped and tore away until he held it to view in the dim light. For a moment he stared at the thing in amazement, and the amazement changed to frenzied horror. With an involuntary scream he sprang to his feet and bounded homeward still clutching his gruesome find.

Running with the swiftness of the fleeting deer he heard breaking dead wood and knew he was pursued. The lone man of the forest had returned, heard Bob's cry of horror and raced in pursuit. A shot went wild, others were imbedded in intervening trees. Flying bullets whizzed by Bob's lowered head. The contestants raced like men at a Marathon – the pursued for his life, the pursuer for the safety of his hideous secret. Once Bob mistakenly rounded an upturned hemlock. It gave the would-be murderer a rod of gain and a clear aim. Instantly came the flash of exploding powder and a ball plowed its way through Bob's right shoulder. The shock of near death lent the youth an added burst of speed. He was unencumbered with his rifle having forgotten it at the moment of his ghastly find, so now he raced in flying leaps until he reached the camp slashing. Here care was required not to enter a labyrinth of piled brush and become helpless target but an intimate knowledge of the logging roads saved him from the fatal chance. At last, faint from the loss of blood, he neared the yellow square of a lamp lighted window, burst open the door and fell headlong on the bunk room floor.

Mann had come over from the mill to scale extra timber being hauled in by farmers. After finishing the job, even to stamping the logs, he had partaken of the supper prepared by Haywire Hank. Hank, having gained a knowledge of cooking during his bachelor experience, had been appointed in Long Jim's place while the remaining teamsters, loaders and rollway men remained in camp. Therefore Tam O'Shanter was peacefully curled up before the fire while Watson, Hilliker, Heald, Sprik and others lighted pipes and discussed the prodigious winter's cut of logs.

"Bob should be back," Mann uneasily commented as minutes slipped by after the evening meal.

"He wouldn't have gone if he knew you needed him at the rollway," Hilliker explained. "He just took a notion to hunt 'fore the mill starts. Might have had an accident with the gun. Carries it careless."

"That's what I'm afraid of," said Mann. "Or that he's lost," he added, thinking of his own dilemma.

As he spoke the door burst in and Bob, wide eyes with terror, fell forward with a crash while his outstretched hand grasped a fragment of rotting cloth that had once been a garment.

Mann and several lumberjacks sprang to the aid of the unconscious youth. Ben Heald and the scaler lifted him to a bench while blood soaked his clothing and dripped to the floor.

"Just what I said," cried Hilliker. "He's awkward with a gun. Shot himself. Might –a bled to death out in them woods and no one the wiser."

"He'll bleed to death now," declared Mann grimly, "if we can't stop this hemorrhage. Jules, take my horse and go for Mrs. Brett as fast as you can ride. Hurry!"

Jules Deveraux bounded for the barn while the scaler attempted to cut away Bob's sleeve from his wound. This increased the danger as the bleeding became a flood yet his clenched hand refused to relinquish his ragged trophy.

"What in thunder is he doing with that cloth?" demanded Heald as Mann tore the fragment from the lad's stiffened clasp. "And where did he get it?" the rollway man asked, curiously eyeing the gray tweed that had once been the lapels and breast of a man's coat.

"Musta been trying to stop his wound." Jim Sprik commented. After that the men forgot everything but the work of first aid.

Before anyone thought it possible Jules returned with Madeline Brett who was wrapped in a long gray cloak, and who immediately took charge of the wounded boy.

With deft, skilled fingers she examined her patient and located the course of the bullet which had plowed its way across the shoulder and upper arm. Quickly the self-taught doctor used a sponge and an antiseptic to clean the wound and applied bandages she had brought with her.

"It's just a flesh wound," Mann remarked with relief. "I suppose there's nothing to fear but blood poison."

"Not that," promised Madeline. "Have him moved to my home and I'll see that he has care while this heals."

She stood erect and glanced about the strange scene. Sitting or standing by the square fireplace were bronzed, roughly clad men of the wilderness. Along each wall extended the double rows of bunks. At her side on benches lay the still unconscious youth whose past and present were both a blank. Beyond him, curiously examining Bob's trophy by lantern light, was Jules Deveraux. He held the cloth aloft to better view the twilled check. On his dark face was a look of amazement that changed to consternation when he saw Madeline step toward him. Instantly he sought to hide the gray cloth from sight, but he was too late.

Before those about her realized the significance of the act she caught the decaying fragment from Jules' hand and uncovered a tarnished lodge pin concealed by the lapel.

"What does this mean?" demanded Mrs. Brett, and in her voice was a shrill note of alarm. "Where did this come from?" Her dark eyes strayed wildly from face to face and fastened on Mann. "Don't you know that coat and pin belonged to Donald?" The marble whiteness of her terrified face left the great eyes contrastingly black and tragic in their intensity. "My God," she cried, "why don't you speak?"

The scaler now comprehended all Bob's find implied and cursed his stupidity. Taking Madeline's shaking hands in his firm grasp he begged her to withhold judgement. But as he sparred for time to collect his thoughts the woman's instinct decided.

"Donald is dead," she affirmed with a shaky voice. "He was murdered," she stated with absolute conviction just above a whisper. Then the reaction from all she had suffered flooded her being like an engulfing tide, drowning her senses. Her swoon was deep and merciful.

"This is a bad business," Hilliker said with an oath. "Everyone o' you'll recollect Brett wore that check suit the last day he was in camp. His wife's right. He was murdered, and like blundering fools we've let her be the one to guess the truth. Now what's to be done?"

Mann told them. "Hilliker, you and I will take Mrs. Brett home in my rig. Watson and Tom Bordon can move Bob. He knew what he'd found, and the shock of it numbed that sick brain, not the gunshot.

"Go ahead," he insisted when Bordon objected to troubling Mrs. Brett with the wounded boy. "She needs Bob. Looking after him may save her from going mad.

"You," he said, turning to Sprik, "better take the blacks and go to Agache for Floyd."

"No, py gar," cried Jules. "Sprik, he keel my horse. I go after heem myself."

"As you like," agreed Mann without pausing in the act of removing Madeline from the suggestive scene. And as Bob Stray showed signs of regaining his shattered senses his attendants hurried him from the bunk room. A short time afterwards Madeline was in Sally's anxious care for the black woman too, learning of the tragedy, feared for her mistress' sanity. Two hours later Floyd arrived and the scaler met him on the porch.

"Tell me all you know and what you suspect," Floyd demanded.

"Bob has made a clear statement," Mann told him. "He found Brett's body and was bringing back proof of it when the assassin attempted his life."

"Whom do you suspect?"

Mann's answer was ready. "Stimson or Nordyke."

Floyd stared at the taller in blank amazement.

"You mistrusted that pair of scoundrels before this," accused the manager. "Why have you kept it to yourself?"

"I had no means of convincing you," Mann told him. "And Bob has no evidence against the murderer. His description of the man by the shallow grave would fit any of a dozen lumberjacks."

"Will Bob be able to lead us to the spot before that ghoul removes traces of the crime?"

"Yes; he'll go if we carry him on a stretcher. He's eager to help, poor lad."

While Mann and Floyd discussed the morning's business another, but vastly different heart to heart was in progress at the Agache boarding house across the road from the Company's store. The flying figure that had pursued Bob ultimately darted northwest by short cuts after losing his prey, then crossed the black and rotten ice of Muskrat Lake, sped along the tram track after reaching the shore and finally arrived in Agache. With the litheness of a prowling cat he shinned up a column of the boarding house porch, raised the front window of Nordyke's room and entered. Nordyke whirled on him with an oath, almost upsetting his lamp.

"Damn you," he hissed. "What devil sent you here?"

"To fix an alibi," Stimson explained breathlessly. "There's another on the list."

"At last," triumphed the bookkeeper.

"Not him," snarled the bush-monkey. "It's the half-wit stamper."

"Of all the infernal fools," snapped Nordyke, "you're it!"

"Listen," commanded his tool. "I went there as you told me to shift them corner stakes. When I got that far I was near it and I thought best to make dead certain no one should blunder onto the grave. It 'u'd set 'em guessing. We didn't -"

"Keep the devilish details to yourself." Cut in Nordyke.

"I was there putting on more dirt and brush about dusk -"

"Make it short," menaced his listener.

"When I reckoned it looked right I loped toward the lake; but before I's gone far I circled back to see there wan't no witness. It was a sure hunch. Something must-a warned me."

"Nonsense," sneered Nordyke. "It was a murderer's curiosity. Go on."

"No names," warned Stimson. "You're as deep in the mud as I am in the mire. Anyhow, I heard a frightened screech and I caught sight of Bob Stray running from -"

"Go on," warned Nordyke.

"I started after him firing every time I got half a chance. He run like a buck. I don't know how many times I hit him. There was a trail of blood. Of course, he's done for."

"Damn you for a blundering fool," hissed the angry bookkeeper. "You've acted the idiot ever since you did for that fellow –"

"Never mind him," interrupted the swamper. "I was a fool all right when I let you use that killing to drive me into your dirty work. Mind, you're in deep as me."

"Shut up. Take these quilts and lie on the floor," Nordyke ordered. He would rather strangle Stimson than room with him; but he was keen enough to appreciate the fine points in the assassin's argument. Also he doubted Bob Stray's demise. Stimson's wild shots might have merely wounded. His victim might live and talk. If so, his story would rouse the whole region. It would be a weird and dangerous task but he and Stimson should hurry to the opened grave and erase every mark. It was the one way to preserve their secret. Yet if Bob lived the place might swarm with lumberjacks, excited and revengeful woodsmen who might inaugurate a lynching bee. His courage vanished. He crept into the bed that lacked its full complement of covering, but he did not sleep.

On the Brett porch Floyd and Mann conversed in low tones.

"This is a frightened ordeal for Mrs. Brett," Mann finally remarked. "She's among strangers. Not a relative to protect her. No one to prosecute the guilty or look out for her interests."

"My friend," Floyd said quietly, "you are blind."

The scaler glanced quickly at the pale earnest face in the lantern glow then responded.

"Yes, I've been blind," he said. "God be with you both."

XVI

Why Mann Learned to Swim

In the cold dawn Bob Stray, supported on horseback and attended by an armed posse of lumberjacks, led the way back over the hills and dales of the forest to the spot where he had surprised the indistinct figure at its dreadful task. Each detail of the imperfect, brush covered grave was exactly as Bob had informed them. But an April mist soaked the workers; and the sight of the place, pain from his wound, his weakened condition and the icy shower combined to make Bob deathly ill. Floyd sent him back to Mrs. Brett with a guard while he and Mann arranged for an interment in the country cemetery, and David Johnathan, who happened to be in the area, conducted the brief ceremony.

All that day Madeline moved like one in a dream. Only Bob's extremity roused her to reasoning activity. Mrs. Jobbin and Mrs. Davitt took charge of the kitchen leaving Sally free to devote herself to her beloved mistress. It was a silent devotion. Madeline was endlessly thinking of her tragedy. She was living in the past. Now that she knew Donald had been true to her and his trust, her relieved heart flooded with tenderness. Months of bitterness were swept away. She found comfort where others expected her to find grief. Donald now represented all that was preeminently noble. Never had she loved and revered him as at present in the character of a martyr. No longer was it necessary to continue the heart breaking struggle of appearing unconcerned at her desertion. All the world would know she had never been cast off as unworthy. She had the right to grieve openly.

"M' pore lil' lamb, m' baby," crooned the black woman who knew Donald Brett's widow experienced the first relief of normal sorrow. That these were the first tears she had shed for <u>him</u>, and not because of shame and wounded pride.

Neighbors vied with one another in offering sympathy. Mrs. Swisher, Mrs. May, Mrs. Coon and others invaded the cook's department with every sort of delicacy for the bereaved wife and sick youth. India Blair came when her increased business permitted. Her strong sane personality routed gloom like sun and a burst of song. Then one morning Sally opened the door in answer to a timid knock and on the portal stood Bob Davitt with a handful of pink arbutus.

"These," he managed to say with a violent blush, "are for my teacher."

At that he held forth in his grimy hands the fragrant, wax-like blossoms, shook his head at Sally's invitation to enter and hastily departed. The boy had fought long with his bashfulness before his reluctant feet dragged him to the Brett threshold with his offering. It was a triumph of mind over matter, but he won in order to show his love and respect for the woman he once vowed to run out of the school in District Number Four.

"Miss Liney," Sally announced as she duly presented the pink nosegay, "dat scalawag ob a Bob Davitt done fetched yo' dese yere posies."

Instantly Madeline caught the fragrant gift to her tear-stained face and, to Sally's distress, broke into unrestrained weeping. Her black nurse mentally railed at herself and Bob Davitt, but invectives would have turned to praise had she known Bob, the young tough, gave her mistress more happiness than all the settlement callers combined. Madeline was aware the boy had walked far to gather his treasure by the lake, that he had mastered boyish shame in showing sentiment and that he braved the possible jeers of Quick and Parsons. So his love was great.

Fickle April deluged the country that night in a final downpour that chilled toward morning into a regal ice storm. Every tree and shrub, encased in an armor of crystal, glittered brilliantly in the sunshine. Pines, unable to bear the weight, drooped in a cascade of glistening beauty while bare branches of beech and maple supported millions of tiny icicles that gave off the tints of a rainbow; and slender willows swept gracefully downward in scintillating glory of jeweled splendor.

"It am jes lak dem walls ob jasper what de Good Book 'scribes in dem scriptures," declared Sam, who was born a poet.

"If de walls o' heaben ain' no mo' lasting 'en dem ice shucks it ain' no use going dar," opined Sally who was nothing if not practical. "Dey would drap quicker 'en de walls ob Jerico widout no blowing ob trumpets or tromping seben times 'round. Whut dey would do is bust first time some onthinking angel played his harp, an' den whar would you be?"

As she spoke the morning breeze swayed the curved branches until their iced tips rattled like castanets. As the sun rose higher and warmed the air millions of glittering shales loosened and fell. Before noon the jewel storm existed only in memory.

Mann and Floyd examined the papers of the late manager, but no amount of search unearthed any source of income for Brett's widow. Brett was not insured in his lodge and what had become of his surplus salary was a mystery as the purchase of his farm home, his driving team and household expenses would not account for the total. The manager's reticence concerning his affairs left everyone, including his wife, absolutely ignorant of his business transactions. This unchanged condition of her finances gave Madeline no concern. She could teach and with Sam's farming they could manage to live. Settlement schools opened for summer terms the first of May, so she would be ready when the time came and welcomed the distraction of employment.

The identity of Brett's murderer, however, ended in suspicion. Chance had almost given Bob Stray this desired knowledge, but that important witness, now fully recovered, was unable to do more than describe a man about the height and spare build of the suspect. Fright, shock at his gruesome discovery and dim light defrauded him of what Brett's friends wished to know.

"We'll wait and watch," decided Floyd.

"That's what I've been doing for months," Mann reminded him. "While we wait there's no knowing what may happen."

"We have no other recourse," said Floyd. "A detective would only skim the surface. He couldn't understand conditions. Now we're two against two. That's something. I wish to God you had trusted me before. I might have helped. Now all we can do is to give the rascal rope enough to hang himself."

"If he don't kill us first," reminded the scaler.

Violent thaw winds broke loose rotting ice on the imprisoned lake and an opening of blue water widened hourly until ice-floes drifted before the gale, pulverized to pencil shapes and piled high on the lee shore. That week the entire surface of Muskrat Lake was dancing water and lumberjacks in hip boots began to break down the rollways and "dog" huge rafts of logs ready for the mill tug, Indian Queen.

Four miles away the Company's mill started into resonant, booming life with its smoke plume varying to the breeze and two circular saws in action day and night. Brinkley bossed the lumber shovers in the mill yard and those who unloaded tram cars at the Lake Michigan pier. From that hour work climaxed to a seeming crescendo of vast confusion.

During long hours Bill Hyde, black haired, black eyed with a double-jointed, back-action temper, stood at the Indian Queen's steering wheel while his one man crew, Bud Hatch, stoked slabs and yelled back curse for taunt. Behind them, millward, trailed sinuous rafts of logs for the greedy boom. To keep a mill crew waiting for logs was unthinkable so Bill Hyde mingled speed and profanity.

Floyd, as manager of triple interests, was constantly on the move. Steel and Hawley depended on him to see that no pause in the involved machinery of their lumbering plant ate up profits. Added to this care was his vigilance in watching Brett's murderer for proof of his crime. Mann, scaling lumber at the pier and in the mill yard, was likewise on the alert to catch the guilty napping.

The much dreaded log-shortage threatened one morning when Brinkley was at his wits end.

"Say, Floyd," he yelled at the manager who chanced to be near. "The pond'll be cleaned out in an hour! If Bill don't bust that biler o' his'n we'll be laid off. Tell him to rush the next tow."

Consequently the manager waited on the slab dock for the arrival of the Indian Queen and her desired raft. On this particular morning the hill-rimmed lake duplicated the budding forest on its burnished surface and reflected the hull of the advancing tug on the calm water.

"Steam up, Bill," Floyd shouted through his funneled hands. "We're short."

At the word Bill Hyde's black head protruded from the wheelroom window and shouted caustic orders to the foreman. In turn a red head uprose from the engine pit and hurled invectives at the captain. The double discharge appeared to have an effect as the tug imperceptibly gained speed until Floyd addressed the men in normal tones.

"For ten days we must rush timber," he told them. "I'll send extra men back with you to the rollways. We must have in logs ahead. Steam up to the limit. Remember you'll get double pay for over time."

"Give me a live engineer," blazed Hyde. "How can I speed up with a dodblasted wooden image in the hold?"

Up from the engine pit popped a smut-blackened face surmounted by tousled red hair.

"Put a man at the wheel," shouted Bud Hatch, "and I'll run 'er like a scart Injun. For double pay I'd chuck that dashed chromo overboard and run her myself. He's naught but a figgerhead."

Sprik and others, waiting to ride the raft into the mill pond laughed uproariously. Captain Hyde's chronic quarrel with his fireman afforded water front amusement but everyone was aware that neither Hyde nor Hatch would work apart.

Floyd disappeared in the direction of the Company's store but was back in an hour with telegraphed orders.

"Take a loading gang to the pier," he told Brinkley. "The Minnetonka is due. Probably will warp in by ten o'clock. It's now nine thirty."

Brinkley immediately summoned a dozen men and started to the big pier with the leisurely deliberation that is typical of timber workers. They found the Minnetonka throwing lines to Pete Gunderson, the dock man while she churned the blue waters of the lake to a foam.

"Load us by night, Brinkley," shouted the barge captain form the deck, "and I'll add a nickel an hour to the men's pay."

"We'll do our best, Captain Gates," the boss assured him.

Men on lumber piles began handing down boards with an easy swing that told of practice while others carried it to the ship's slide and passed it down to men in the hold. Mann tallied the shipment as pile after pile was swallowed by the insatiable maw of the freighter. Before the hold and decks had stored the last board possible a brilliant sun burned down the western sky into the rippling lake that flamed like a sea of fire. It was so glorious a panorama the scaler stood admiring the scene long after crew and dock man had gone to their delayed supper. At his right glimmered the early lights of Agache through its sheltering grove of pine, at his left the long curve of the yellow beach. Not a sound marred the witchery of the hour but the soft lapping of water against the wharf; certainly not the stealthy foot fall of a form inching toward him in the gathering twilight. With lynx tread the skulking figure crossed the intervening space between the freight house and the remaining lumber pike. Then he made a silent rush and planted two forceful palms between the shoulders of the dreamer. Instantly the scaler shot forward and down into two fathoms of water before he could utter a cry or realize what had occurred. Above him on the pier Stimson peered over the edge to observe the success of his maneuver. It was all he could wish, so he picked up his shoes by the freight house, rushed down the pier into the grove where he dressed his feet then sped on until he mingled with barge loaders in the Company's store. No one guessed he had not been with them from the moment they gathered about the office wicket to receive their loading checks. He moved from group to group making certain that, welcome or not, the men observed his presence. Ridman, joking with purchasers, handed out tobacco and whipped cord about parcels with his usual dexterity.

"Hello, Stimson," he jollied the bush-monkey. "Been moon gazing?"

The chance shot sent Stimson swearing to Nordyke's office where the bookkeeper glanced at his accomplice with slightly elevated brows. It was a query the swamper answered with a nod. At that moment the last barge loader approached, received his check and departed whereupon Nordyke made out an additional slip and handed it to Stimson.

"Now go," he flashed, "Get out among the man. Keep out of my office."

Sullenly Stimson obeyed, and joined a number setting out for Buck Bender's saloon. They found this malodorous resort swarming with lumberjacks intent upon having Bender cash checks in return for a certain amount of patronage over the bar. Two card tables were in full swing and in the corner crouched Jim Sprik too drunk to sit upright and too sober for removal to a rear room because he vigorously objected.

Ben Heald, Watson, Bateman, Hilliker and Davitt handed checks to the saloon keeper and were accommodated with currency less the amount of their score. Haywire Hank strode to the bar and handed out a slip which Bender cashed. But to the amazement of Bender and the spectators Hank coolly pocketed his money with the exception of a coin which he pushed toward the saloonist.

"That there's for your brother," he explained.

"Set up drinks, you tightwad," several lumberjacks yelled at him. "Loosen up."

The remark roused Sprik. His booze-inflamed intellect saw justifiable grounds for battle. With a bound he was at Hank's elbow and placed a blow that almost knocked the astonished top-loader to the floor.

"That's to teach you manners," Sprik yelled. "No one but a damned hog 'u'd forget the drinks."

"By Judas, you swilled down more now then you orter, an' I ain't going to make no whiskey jug out o' you," squeaked Hank in his rising and falling treble. He quietly shoved Jim back but the young lumberjack began to fight desperately, calling on Davitt for aid. Davitt at once responded but his object was pacific. He tried to drag his friend back to his corner until he became sober or peacefully drunk. His act was misunderstood and the combatants redoubled their efforts – Sprik supposing he was assisted and Hank believing he confronted two opponents. In the fury of the three way contest the actors caromed against Stimson and with blind impartiality Sprik aimed a blow at the swamper's head, following up with a vicious punch in the stomach. Stimson, dizzy with pain, let loose the vials of his wrath.

"Let me be, damn you," he shouted at Davitt. "If you don't you're likely to need that nigger doctor again and this time it'll be for a broken head."

At the insulting word Bat Davitt's fighting instinct routed his new born desire for peace. With a rush he dealt a blow that dropped Stimson like a nine-pin and the swamper's downfall upset the card table, scattering the cards and bringing the players to their feet. Davitt's healed limb was bent above Stimson's chest while his gnarled hands reached for the swamper's throat; but to his amazement the bush-monkey's ferret eyes gazed past him with the expression of abysmal horror and the man's face bleached to wax. Instinctively Davitt looked up to see what disturbing object was focused by his victim's staring eyes and saw nothing more noteworthy than Forrest Mann. The scaler had entered the room and stood watching the fight as if keenly interested in the results. His clothing was wet. He looked like one who had walked in heavy rain. Davitt turned to his captive and bestowed some vitriolic advice.

"If I ever hear that word from you again you'll need a wooden overcoat. Remember!"

Davitt stood up, and Sprik whirled back from Hank, the perspiring victor.

"Noew," said Hank with convincing emphasis, "I's a-going to set and rest m'self; and I ain't going to buy no gol darn likker lesson I have a mind to." Which program he carried out with no further interference. Even Sprik made no comments concerning Haywire Hank's stubborn policy of abstinence.

Stimson, however, continued to stare at the astonishing apparition that confronted him. He was well aware that Mann was unable to swim yet here the scaler stood by Bender's bar drinking a hot sling and apparently none the worse for his plunge off the long pier.

The explanation of the tally man's appearance was exceedingly matter of fact. He managed to clasp the slimy base of a pile as he came to the surface after being hurled in the lake. To climb upward on the water-soaked timber was impossible and his water-soaked clothing slowly dragged him downward. With grim despair he clung to his treacherous support and shouted and shouted for help. No one heard him, and with death barely minutes away in water that still had the tang of winter ice Mann bitterly regretted that swimming had been omitted from his athletic course.

He was too much in love with life – and India Blair – to die needlessly. Absorbing interests claimed his attention. He wanted to live more than he desired life hereafter yet, with his mind active and his body vigorous, he seemed hopelessly doomed. Of course he knew the author of his misfortune. There was but one man in that region capable of the peculiar treachery. That man was Stimson, tool of Nordyke.

Helplessly sinking he sent forth call after call for chance assistance. No one was likely to hear. Agache was too far distant. Only a straggler is the grove might come to his aid and that was one chance in ten thousand.

As water rose to his throat he caught the sound of oars evenly smiting the lake and creaking in their locks. The muffled screech renewed his courage and tensed his hold on the slimy pile. Nearer the lone boatman approached until Mann's call for help reached him above the whine of oars and his own song of the sea. The oarsman was a huge, powerful, white haired fisherman with merry blue eyes and the rolling gait of a salt water sailor. Fish, pronounced feesh, was his main diet, his chief revenue and his topic of conversation. This night his errand was to secure a fresh supply of salt at Agache so that no time of the following day might be wasted. Therefore Uncle Joe was leisurely pulling his fish boat toward the source of supplies while he enjoyed the night. The startling shout of someone apparently under the Company's dock brought him cumbersomely around the end of the pier and within sight of the almost drowning scaler.

"My God, young feller," he ejaculated, "you'll get colt alretty! W'y don't you swim?"

"I can't," Mann admitted with teeth chattering. "But if you'll help me this time I promise you there won't be a next time."

XVII

India Blair's Suitors

Bob Stray's convalescence soon became robust health. Aunt Sally's wholesome cooking and Madeline's unceasing care brought about the desired effect. It was of value to both since Madeline benumbed her grief in ceaseless ministrations. The boy's loss of memory roused her interest. She read and studied everything bearing on brain trouble until she became convinced a slight operation would restore the lad to mental health. A surgeon might open the closed door of Bob's past. When she finally talked with him of this possibility his clear eyes grew misty with hope and gratitude.

"I'd go through anything for a chance," he declared. "The big thing in my life will be to know – to remember who I am."

"When you are entirely strong," Madeline told him, "we'll have Dr. Monroe over at the bay lift that bit of a depressed bone above your temple. It may help. At least it won't harm."

When Forrest Mann was told of Mrs. Bret's design he remarked with hearty approval.

"I wish we'd thought of that before."

Keenly he once more studied the high bred face that was persistently familiar. Unbidden the thought came that the restoration of Bob's memory might prove disastrous to himself, but he'd remain at his post as long as possible to convict Stimson of murder and Nordyke of guilty knowledge. Bob came first. He would not delay the operation a day even if the worst results to himself ensued.

The summer term of school opened and Madeline walked each day amid scenes of rural beauty. The callow foliage of the great forest was yellow while hepaticas, squirrel-corn and flaming adder tongue preceded the blossoming of myriads of trilliums. Wild plum and cherry blossoms made gay the roadside while velvet green meadows and lawns were tightly buttoned to earth by countless yellow dandelions.

Jud Coon was right when he predicted the summer school would prove a snap. The larger boys and many of the older girls were employed on the farms but a few new pupils came from distant homes. Zoe Higbee was the one discordant note. Bereft of the masculine admiration she craved, her time was openly frittered away while she lolled in her seat and dreamed of future conquests. Lily May, however applied herself with diligence. Her ambitious object was to pass the fall examination and teach a winter school, so Madeline aided her by extra lessons at her home.

Small orchards burst into pink and white blooms that gave place to early fruit and a riot of roses in settlement gardens reminded Lily of the near holiday with its day time picnic and evening ball at Agache.

"I do wish," Lily confided to Madeline one evening as they walked from school under the canopy of lush green, "that I owned a pretty dress for the Fourth of July dance. I never had a real nice dress in my life." The red lips drooped, the innocent blue eyes were wistful.

"Come home with me," Madeline offered, "and I'll cut over one of my white lawns. I'll never use it," she assured her favorite pupil. "If you wish we'll go to your place and ask permission of your mother."

"Oh, Mrs. Brett," cried Lily, her blue eyes shining, "you don't know how I've <u>longed</u> for a white dress!"

The two, teacher and pupil, turned into a woods path that led to the May farm. About them was dense forest in which a vireo trilled his early evening song, whirling waves of melody and at the May clearing a scarlet tanager darted past them like a spurt of flames. Lordly robins executed little runs and black cowbuntings hovered about gaunt boned, grazing bossies.

Mrs. May, bare arms akimbo and suds soaked apron advertising her employment, met them at the door of their log house, listened to Lily's request and readily gave her pleased consent.

"Lil ain't had no chance to make nothin' of herself, Mis' Brett," declared the doting mother. "I'm thankful you favor her. She's my pride, Lil is. My boys ain't much at learnin' and I don't look to 'em, but my Lil's going to turn out splendid."

"About this ball," hesitated Madeline. "Is it all right?"

"Lil's crazy to go," said Mrs. May. "It's can't do her no harm. All the best folks are there – Miss Blair, the store clerks and bookkeeper besides Mr. Floyd and the scaler. An' Lil goes with her brothers. She's well cared for."

Being thus assured that all was as it should be Madeline took Lily home with her and plunged into the delightful task of converting her lace-trimmed frock into a ravishing gown for the country girl who watched the transformation with absorbing interest.

At last the dainty costume was completed and Lily, trembling with happy excitement, dressed in her first white gown. When she stepped forth for the artist and Aunt Sally to view the result the black woman exclaimed:

"Good lan', dat chile don't look human!"

It was equivocal praise, but Lily was an angelic vision. Her sunny hair was tied with ribbons of the same azure as her dancing eyes. The rose flush on her dimpled cheeks accented the pure white of her satiny throat and bare arms. She was slenderly graceful and wonderfully beautiful in the manner of an exquisite flower by moonlight.

"Looks jes' lak yo' coming out party rig, Miss Liney," declared the cook. "Jes lak an angel outen de glory lan'."

Madeline's delighted gaze expressed her pleasure. She caught the lovely vision in her arms and kissed the dimpling cheek.

"My dress is grand, Mrs. Brett," cried Lily, tearfully grateful. "I'm so happy over the beauty of it I could die."

"Nonsense," laughed Madeline. "You'll want to live and enjoy it."

As an accompaniment to her words the evening stillness was broken by the weird call of a whip-poor-will and the far off reply of his distant mate. Again and again he swiftly uttered Whip-poor-will!

Whip-poor-will! And afar the faint refrain, Whip-poor-will! Whip-poor-will! Whip! Ending on the first syllable with a snap.

"Hear dat?" demanded Sally. "Hear dat bird o' il omen chucklin' ober comin' misery to some poor soul?"

"Nonsense," again ejaculated Madeline. "That night bird is as innocent of evil as a robin."

At the Blair home a party dress similar in hue to Lily May's but garnished with ribbons of cardinal, awaited its owner's pleasure. India, however, was still busy with her mill accounts. They were multiple and intricate since the Blair cut was towed across Muskrat Lake on scows, shifted to the Company's pier on the tram cars and shipped on barges to market. In addition to pay roll for her mill crew she now had bills for scowing, hauling and dockage. Her dark eyes scanned columns of figures with accurate speed, but her subconscious mind was employed on a different problem. She wondered if this night of the holiday ball would bring to Mann's lips the words she longed to hear. His so named "accident" on the deserted dock frightened her as told volubly by Uncle Joe, the fisherman who saved his life. Despite the scaler's attempt to make her think the incident trivial she divined the truth and all the tenderness of her intense nature went out to him in devotion. Unreservedly she was his and she determined that nothing in heaven or on earth should keep them apart. If he would only speak. Why was he silent? His strange aloofness was unaccountable knowing beyond doubt that he loved her.

Having finished her accounts India craved the open air and walked slowly toward the river. The hour was early and she wanted to be alone. There was ample time for a stroll before dressing for the evening's entertainment. The liquid trill of a thrush singing his whirling song soothed her spirit. The rushing river, pouring through its gorge between hills, gleamed like a ribbon of silver and reflected overhanging cedars in rich shadows. For a time India watched the sliding sheen of water until a step roused her from an almost hypnotic trance. She looked up and saw that Nordyke, faultlessly groomed and darkly handsome, stood near the river path.

"The scene – and you – are enchantingly attractive," he smiled. "But I came to see the jewel, not the setting."

In that moment India knew by the expression of Nordyke's black eyes what was coming and would have escaped if possible. The bookkeeper barred the way. He had followed her along the narrow way determined to declare his passion since chance had favored him, so he plunged into a proposal of marriage in words that came rapidly, forcefully.

"I've waited months," he said in conclusion, "for this opportunity. You must know that I'd give my immortal soul for your favor. Don't answer now," he hastily objected. "Wait! Don't wrong us both. Withhold your decision until you've considered every point involved. I've waited long, and I can wait longer – for happiness."

He must have observed furious anger welling in India's great eyes and heard her emphatic denial of his suit. But he turned without appearing to listen and disappeared around a bend in the river.

That night the hall above the Company's store filled early. Windows were opened to the soft, July air. Fabrics of light material and bright tints were as much an expression of the season as the banks of flowers decorating every available place. Already the home talent orchestra was in spirited action, and Hod Elwin called off for the dancers while he observed new arrivals at the near-by stair head. Presently his eyes lighted with admiration as India Blair, in white linen with a sash and trimmings of cardinal silk, came up the steps in company with Forrest Mann. The scaler with his grave eyes of darkest blue, had never appeared to better advantage as India noted with a contented sense of ownership. She was glad this man loved her but wrath flushed her handsome face because another dared to approach while this lover dallied.

When Walter Nordyke entered the dance hall he glanced about for India and wonderer if his business-like wooing would have immediate reward. Surely the mill girl would see that her affairs needed his remarkably capable hand. He knew India loved success. In time she'd summon him to straighten out the Blair difficulties, and he'd arrange that there were many of them. The flash of her scornful eyes had not promised hope, but the girl was no fool and he looked forward with confidence to her decision.

Then his roving gaze encountered Lily May and his black brows elevated with amazement. It was hard to realize that this exquisite vision was the shrinking, timid child he had favored with attention. At once he moved to her side and requested a dance. His satanic eyes devoured Lily's wild rose beauty and his lips uttered extravagant words of praise. The girl's long lashes drooped before his ardent love making, but her cheeks dimpled with smiles. Never before in her brief life had she been so deliriously happy. Her black eyed lover lavished endearments but he said nothing of a future. Lily, however, believed herself fortunate to have gained the devotion of one so eminently above herself and supposed, simple child, that his love was as enduring as her own.

"She's like the roses at her waist," mused Nordyke. "Lovely tonight but hideous with age."

This night India Blair could not altogether avoid the bookkeeper. The violins had struck up a rhythmic waltz when he approached and peremptorily requested her favor, and she had no ready excuse. Next moment they were keeping step. But Nordyke found it extremely difficult to sentimentally embrace the girl lumberjack who proved as unyielding as a mischievous colt. But the nearness of India's proud, flushed face, the flash of her splendid eyes, the vitality emanating from her lithesome form hurried him to indiscretion.

"I must know tonight if you will marry me," he insisted.

"Never," she flung back as they reversed in the waltz. "You know that."

"But I love you," he urged. "I adore you, queen of women. And you need me."

"Understand once and for all that what you ask will never be."

"Better take a man who urges his suit," flared Nordyke, "than wait for one who doesn't know his mind."

India looked into her partner's eyes, and laughed. The laugh was insolent, defying.

"When I wish to marry you, Mr. Nordyke," she said curtly, "I'll send for you."

With that she disengaged herself from his clasp, nodded and was gone, leaving him alone on the floor.

"You'll send for me all right," he hissed after her. "I swear it."

When the girl mill owner and her escort started homeward the lake lay like burnished silver in the gray dawn. It seemed unreal, a vision of something let down from heaven rather than earthly. No sounds broke the night's calm save the organ-bass of frogs in shallow swales but India's thoughts were not in harmony. She was furious at the man who asked her hand in marriage for financial reasons, and at herself for wishing the dilatory lover at her side to speak. Mann sensed her mood without guessing the cause therefore found less trouble than he anticipated in keeping himself in hand.

At the gate India bade him good night and sought her room with her usually clear mind in a whirl of conflicting emotions. She raged at Nordyke for suspecting her secret, and was angry with the scaler for not putting her in a position to refute the bookkeeper's insulting statement. Unwittingly Mann had, according to settlement custom, committed himself to either marry or be refused. He had singled her out for attention, and "kept company" with her. She was mystified by his strange silence and she resolved to end their association. She appreciated Mann's nobility and big hearted kindness but she refused to be a target for settlement gossip.

XVIII

The Fire

That summer was what the settlers considered the hottest in seven years. A pitiless glare of sunshine followed a July drought and slashings dried to tinder. Sun heat baked the earth until crops withered and highways sent up smothering clouds of dust after disturbing wheels. Everywhere sounded the rasp of devouring locusts while cicada shrilled in tree tops.

During a day of extreme heat Floyd was summoned some miles into the country concerning a desirable tract of timber offered to the firm through Nordyke. The manager was obliged to look it over and decide upon a price. At the Brett home he picked up Phil and the two drove east with the sweating team at a walk. About them the hot air shimmered like pulsating heat from a furnace. Fields on either hand appeared to be struck by a blight, the shrill of insects was eloquent of intolerable drought.

"If fires start they'll sweep the country," Floyd declared with an anxious gaze at the drooping landscape.

"Heat usually brings rain," said Phil. "This should end in a thunder shower," he decided hopefully.

Their way led past the camp's slashing, then over a succession of hills to the rear line of the township. Foam flecked the sides of their lagging bays when they sighted the farm of Matt Tucker whom the manager was to interview. Tucker, arrayed for comfort in a calico shirt with sleeves rolled to the elbow, jean overalls and a straw hat stuffed with green leaves for protection from sunstroke, came forward to meet them.

"Me sell a forty!" he ejaculated when Floyd made known his errand. He stood with feet planted wide apart and his perspiring face a picture of sheer astonishment. "Not by a long shot. I had Mandy write that skinflint of a bookkeeper my land was my own for keeps. I said tell that leech when I'd a mind to make a present of it to Steel and Hawley we'd tell him the news."

"Do I understand you to say I'm not expected to appraise that timber?" Floyd demanded, amazed and angry. "Didn't you send for me?"

"Not by a jugful," Tucker assured him, and spat to emphasize his denial.

It was an exasperating situation and Floyd wanted to get back to Agache and clear it up; but the overheated team must eat and rest, and the hospitable Tucker insisted that the Floyds partake of new potatoes and peas, besides other wholesome viands, before returning. When finally on the way a western breeze cooled the air but was stifling with drifting smoke from some forest fire. The pungent odor thickened as they proceeded and at the camp slash they entered a gray haze that stung their eyes and filled their lungs. The Brett farm lay under a smoke cloud and Sam, wide eyed with terror, informed them that the woods beyond the Blair mill was in flames.

"Then," said the manager, "nothing can save it."

Leaving Phil with explicit directions to guard the Brett house from fire he took Sam with him to drive the jaded team back from the lake. At the shore, near the depleted rollways, he alighted and started across the lake in a row boat. His object was twofold. He wished to learn if help had been sent to protect the Blair holdings and note Nordyke's attitude in the matter. Dark suspicion took possession of his harassed mind. His fool's errand, this immediate holocaust, the log spiking, Brett's murder and the attempts on the scaler's life welded together in one chain of correlated disaster. He had not wasted time seeking help to row to the Company's gang-saw mill because he knew every man near Blair's would be at the front of the blazing fire-wall. That to him explained the absence of men on the Steel and Hawley rollways. They had quit dogging rafts to help fight fire. As he flung wide, deep strokes of his oars he could see flames licking up timber and brush along the south bluff while a pall of smoke shut out the heavens and gave a lurid cast to the sun now setting afar over the sand dune. Near the slab dock he found the Indian Queen at anchor but with steam up and Bill Hyde leaning over the side engaged in savage profanity. The roar of machinery at the mill proved that the night gang had gone on duty.

"Why hasn't our mill crew joined the fire fighters?" demanded Floyd when he could make himself heard."

"Waiting orders," Bill retorted.

"Men don't need orders in a case like this," shouted the manager angrily.

"Mr. Floyd," Bill explained, "we've had orders from the only other man in authority an' he told us the fire wan't none o' our damned business and to keep away from it or lose our jobs."

"You mean Nordyke?" queried the manager, eyes blazing.

"He's the jigger," admitted Bill. "But thinking your ideas might be contrary I kept up steam 'stead of tying up for the night."

"Sound the emergency call," the manager commanded. "And keep it going."

Joyfully reached for the whistle cord and sent forth long, reverberating blasts that brought two score waiting men from the boarding house on the run. They had in fact been listening for the signal.

"You see they was ready, Mr. Floyd," Bill commented dryly. "Didn't dare to act without your backing. They have families an' Nordyke threatened to fire 'em if they went; an' none o' them could stand for two fires."

"Where's Mann?" asked Floyd.

"Went hours ago with Bob Stray," someone answered. "He saw the fire and skipped right lively."

"He ain't put it out," observed Hyde with a wave of his arm at the flame-swathed hills. Hyde's ironic remark referred to raging fire in an area to be estimated by five miles of city streets and a width no one could measure. As darkness gathered the south shore appeared like a cone of continuous flame punctuated by fire-tongues that shot upward.

"Rush the old tub," besought Watson of the engineer.

"Whoop 'er up," demanded Sprik of the dark gnome in the pit, and peering down was amazed to see an extra man shoving slabs in the fire box whose brick red hair matched Bud's and whose red gums grinned widely identifying him as Guy, the camp chore boy. He was aiding Hatch to coax every ounce of speed from the ancient boiler and engine. But Captain Hyde added his expostulations to the impatient shouts of swarming volunteers.

"Why don't you get up steam, you dashed, wall-eyed pike?" he yelled through the speaking tube. "Think this here's a funeral? Think you're driving a hearse? Think we're a passel o' mourners?"

"You'll be the corpse," came back from the engine-pit, "and there won't be no mourners if you don't shut your dod-blasted mouth when she's eating down slabs like a hawg in a corn patch."

Guy fed slabs into the fire-box like hoecake to a starving dog, and both he and Bud looked black as Charon driving a new sort of steam craft across the river Styx with shadowy passengers leaning over the rail. Finally they neared the spark-showering range, anchor was cast and a landing boat began to carry men, shovels, axes and pails to the fire-rimmed shore.

"Go to the front," Floyd commanded, "and send back the Blair crew; Hilliker and Brinkley tell me the only chance is to back-fire. If we do that they'd be caught like rats in a trap."

"All right," agreed Davitt, who was addressed.

"Use the skiff for speed and take Sprik. Tell them to count their men. No one must be left behind. It would mean death."

"We'll get every man out," promised Davitt. A half mile down the shore the two men landed and sought those who had been vainly contending against the fiery element. One by one they discovered the Blair crew with grimed faces working like fiends in an inferno. Occasionally a pine top burst into leaping flame that added to the steady light of ground fires on which fighters threw shoveled earth. Balsam, the sawyer, and Shawnoga, the Indian, were the first they encountered.

"Floyd brought forty Steel and Hawley men, and they're going to back-fire," shouted Sprik. "Get out!"

"Ought-a done it before," shrilled Balsam. "That's what we want but we ain't got enough men to risk putting a fire line nearer the mill."

"It's being done now," yelled Sprik. "Count your men and get them out on the run."

"There's about a dozen besides three rollway 'jacks. We'll round them up. You and Davitt can go back and get at the fire line."

At the scene of action Floyd's men were vigorously falling an abatis across the course of the oncoming fire. Trees were felled with tops toward the expected blaze while others spaded a trench of fresh earth. Torches at once set the abatis in crackling flames and fifty men of both mill crews watched every brand that threatened the unburned area which contained the Blair mill and logs. Farther on were the Steel and Hawley rollways but the river flowed by them on the fire side making them safe, and Floyd understood Nordyke's inaction. His interests were not in danger.

Beyond the abatis trees turned in a twinkling to giant torches as fire seized a dead hemlock or pitch-filled pine. Flames flung to the breeze in lurid banners while above the red forest boomed the indescribable roar of a vast holocaust. The two fire walls were but rods apart that rapidly narrowed as creeping fire licked up brush and seemed to even burn the earth.

Out of the smoke gloom moved forms of men and women carrying pails of water to the workers and the refreshing liquid was eagerly quaffed, sponged into smarting eyes or poured over hot clothing as firemen entered the zone of intolerable heat. One of the water carriers was India. Her dark face was set and stern, her large eyes were deeply underscored by heart breaking anxiety. She was here, there, everywhere watching the progress. Her business costume of corduroy was soiled by smut and smoke. She was wearied to exhaustion yet active with the strength of excitement.

"Where is Mann?" she asked Bat Davitt, knowing he recalled her mill crew from the danger strip.

"I don't know," said Davitt. "Was he in there with the Blair men?"

"Where's the scaler?" she next demanded of Balsam.

"I don't know," said Balsam. "Isn't he with Floyd's crew?"

India sped toward the lake and encountered Floyd in the flare of a blazing cedar.

"Where's Mann" she asked, repeating her monotonous query.

"I don't know," as monotonously answered the manager. "Isn't he with Balsam?"

India waited for no more. At the lake she launched the skiff. It offered safety if fire drove her from the woods. Past the backfire she rowed until she reached the meeting fire-wall. Here she landed and entered the smoke-filled interval. The place was stifling and dark so she turned toward the light of scorching flame in order to see her way. The advancing fire moved unevenly and she rounded red points or dipped into bay-like recesses. Sometimes she trod on turf that smoldered but bravely she groped onward calling one name,

"Forrest! Oh, Forrest!"

The crash of falling timber mingled with her warning shout. Choking, stumbling she at last found him in blinding smoke unaware that he was alone, but stubbornly defending the line to which he had been assigned.

"My God, India, this is no place for you," he shouted, waving her back.

"Nor for you," cried India, and burst into hysterical laughter.

"We're both in danger," she told him as her nerves steadied, and explained the situation. "Come! We may manage. But it's fifty rods to the lake."

As she spoke Mann could see the eastern wall of flame glowing through the darkness like street lights in a fog. Realization of what India had dared in risking her life roused him to impatient anger.

"Why did you?" he demanded roughly as with an arm flung about her he rushed her toward the distant beach. "You must have been mad." He groaned.

They were forced to pause. A pillar of fire that had been a huge hemlock, tottered and fell across their path. The glare lighted their faces, revealed the grime on clothing and flesh, also the depth of despair in Mann's blue eyes and the glory of great love in the dark ones of the girl lumberjack.

"Because," she answered him with her face close to his lips, "I'd rather die here and now with you than to go out alone."

"Oh, my dear one, my love," he cried, clasping her close to his wildly throbbing heart. "You don't know what you say! You don't know what I am! I've been a coward. India, India, my love, I am not fit to approach you even in friendship. I am an escaped convict."

XIX

Bob Remembers

It was an hour after the lovers escaped from the inferno of meeting fires that Floyd observed Mann working at the front which now, escaping control, threatened to do its worst. The scaler's face was haggard and blackened and his clothing scorched. As he began to shovel sand on a flying brand he felt rain. A low growl of thunder grumbled across the heavens that split with lightening.

"Rain," cried Floyd. "The danger's over!"

"Not yet," said Mann. "Not while Nordyke's devilish cunning points the way. The fire was incendiary. I'm sure of it. I noticed Stimson's absence from the mill. The fact disturbed me knowing the pair might be at their next move – as they were. By the time I located Stimson the mischief was done. He had been across the narrows bridge on a trumped up errand. In half an hour I saw the south woods were blazing and the fire running before a west wind."

"While I was tricked on a fool's errand," raged Floyd, and related his day's experience.

"You can't corner him. He'll say he misunderstood. Stimson will swear he had nothing to do with the fire. They're slippery as eels," declared Mann. He now bared his mind concerning the bookkeeper and his tool. He gave the true significance of his plunge from the pier and his fear for India's safety. But he said nothing of the despairing minutes he and India were imprisoned between the fire-walls or their terrible flight among showering embers and through furnace heat to the cool lake. Neither did he confide to the manager his long kept secret. India had pleaded for delay assuring him of her absolute confidence in his integrity. As a last argument she reminded him that his task of bringing the guilty to justice was not finished.

"It will be," he grimly promised. "And when that precious pair are headed for the penitentiary I escaped from I'll gladly resume my place as Number 709. It will end the suspense of always being on guard.

Two days after the fire Dr. Monroe arrived at Madeline Brett's for the purpose of operating on Bob Stray. His light driving team showed signs of much day and night work as the doctor practiced medicine as well as surgery and had patients in an astonishingly wide area. He was a big man physically and otherwise and his genial presence aided his cures. His deep, mellow voice and his large, assured manner inspired confidence as he now talked with Madeline and studied Bob Stray.

"This contusion," he decided when he examined Bob's head, "is comparatively slight. All it needs is the simplest trepanning and the young man won't be inconvenienced a week."

Dr. Monroe had already been acquainted with every detail of the boy's known history. He was likewise aware that Madeline would be efficient aid to him during the surgical work and that her home would provide a good substitute hospital in a region destitute of such a convenience. He improvised an operating table, sterilized his instruments and began anesthetizing his anxious patient. Mann, at Madeline's request, was on hand in case of necessity. But the work proceeded smoothly and when the last stitch was taken in the scalp and the bandage applied the three put Bob to bed to sleep off his narcotic.

"Give him non-stimulating food," directed the surgeon. "Keep him quiet for a few days, then send for the friends he names and let him go home." This was the doctor's last and only advice.

After Bob's drugged sleep ended he opened drowsy eyes and wonderingly regarded Madeline in the soft light of his shaded room.

"My head aches like a sore tooth, nurse," he remarked. The words told Madeline that the operation was a success for the boy evidently supposed himself in a hospital. He imagined the black clad, white aproned woman by his bed was a trained nurse, and he did not recognize her as Mrs. Brett! She rejoiced. His illusion helped her to insist on sleep, and more sleep interspersed with beaten eggs in milk and savory soups.

"Where am I?" he began to demand. "I never saw this sanitarium before. And it's darned funny my folks don't come, or send word, any more that if I'd cracked a safe. What ails them?"

"No more talking," hushed Madeline. "You've been ill and we want you to rest. Stop thinking. Go to sleep."

Later Bob was permitted to lie on the sitting room couch and dine from a tray. More and more he stared in sheer bewilderment at – to him – new people. His nurse dared not excite him by the truth – that about two years had been erased from his mind as if they had never been. Floyd called but the invalid glanced up as at a stranger and politely acknowledged Madeline's introduction to the manager. Sally, coming and going with trays, puzzled him.

"That cook's a jim dandy," he praised. "Gets up uncommon grub for a hospital of this size. Must be a long way out of Dearborn. Rest cure I suppose. But my folks needn't spread themselves. I just got jarred a bit. But how I lost my wits until they moved me here is a joke."

He put up a hand and felt his bandaged head.

"Sore yet," admitted. "I expect Dad will go on fierce about that game. He hates football anyhow."

Floyd and Madeline exchanged glances of amazement. So that was the explanation. Bob had been injured in a game of football! They refrained from questions as much depended on the boy's tranquility of mind. Moreover Floyd was due at the mill yard where Mann was tallying the growing piles of lumber that came from the gang saws faster than it could be shipped.

Thinking of Bob Stray's pitiful case Floyd drove toward Agache and thus met the bookkeeper in his handsome rig. The two men nodded greeting although neither pretended liking for the other. Nordyke hated Floyd on the principle that causes Satan to dislike baptismal fluid, and the manager considered Nordyke a potential murderer. At the south end of the bridge the bookkeeper turned eastward along the fire-scarred bluff, and as he surveyed the blackened forest his handsome face darkened with rage, his black eyes flashed.

"The meddling fool," he angrily mused. "I wish Stimson had tied a stone on his devilish neck before he bounced him in the lake."

It added nothing to Nordyke's peace of mind to drive by the booming, screeching Blair mill that should have burned to ashes and so have ended its activity. But he silently moved on past the Brett farm and finally stopped under wide spreading trees where a well-trodden path led toward the May dwelling. Here he tied his horse and walked a few paces along the beaten track.

"Why did the white faced simpleton appoint daylight for our meeting?" he muttered. "Well, it's the first and last. I'll end this complaining. I'm sick of the whining fool."

A step drew near and Mrs. May with her large, fair countenance violently flushed and her eyes red with weeping, approached around a bend in the path. At sight of her Nordyke retreated to his carriage and stood by the wheel waiting.

"I've come in Lil's place," the woman said in utterance thick with despair. "I come to ask you to marry her. You know why. Tell me if you will do right by my girl. Will you give her an honest name?"

"I won't be driven," snapped Nordyke. "I refuse to bargain with anyone but the girl."

He loosened his horse's tie strap and stepped into the rig. "And the bargain isn't marriage; it's money. I was to see her today. This is a trap."

"Tomorrow," urged the half crazed mother, catching the wheel's rim in her convulsive grasp. "Marry her tomorrow when David Johnathan comes to preach!"

"No," denied the man harshly. "But I'll talk with the girl exactly as I agreed. Tell her to be here tomorrow at this hour, but no fooling mind. I'll not deal with you or any of the family." He struck the horse a vicious blow but the distracted woman caught the reins and dragged the animal back on its haunches.

"My God, you can't mean it," she cried. "For sake of the mother who bore you have mercy. Think of my child!"

Another blow of the whip sent the frightened beast from the spot and left the frenzied mother weeping and wringing her hands.

"The boys'll kill him," she whimpered. "There'll be no end of trouble. But that won't save my girl, my poor Lil. God, how can we bear this grief and shame?"

The bookkeeper returned to Agache by a leisurely detour around the north side of the lake. He was in an unenviable mood which was not improved by catching sight of Mann and Floyd just leaving the village on their way to Bob Stray's supposed sanitarium. It was the first time the scaler had called on Bob since his operation and he was mentally braced for a recognition that might sweep away his chance of continuing espionage over Stimson.

Bob looked up as they entered the Brett sitting room with its snowy curtains and cheerful interior. At once the youth's delicate countenance lighted with relief. Is expression showed the joy an alien exhibits at the welcome face of a familiar face.

"Franklin Manning, you're here!" he exclaimed, catching the scaler's hand in a hearty grip.

"Yes," said the scaler. His expression was a study, and the other stared in amazement as he continued. "You were here when I came," he told Bob, "and your face has puzzled me. Even now I can't recall your name or where I have before seen you."

"No wonder," cried Bob. "You never spoke to me in your life, but I saw you many a time in the paying teller's cage at the Union Bank. I was a messenger and of course handed my sealed packets to Park Cutler, receiving teller. My name is Jack Wylie and my folks live on Euclid Avenue."

"So you're the bank runner who dealt with Cutler," mused Manning, whose name had received an extra syllable.

"That's why I never talked with you," said Jack Wylie. "But I liked you and was awfully sorry when all that happened about you being arrested when Cutler was the thief."

"What!" cried Manning. "Who said Cutler was the thief?"

"He did," said Jack. "Thought he was dying after being smashed in a train wreck and confessed."

"I was not aware," Manning quietly observed, "that Cutler ever admitted his guilt."

"Last week the papers told the whole story," said Jack. "Everybody knows you let them send you up to save the president's son because Cutler befriended you. Regular spread eagle toot. Didn't you read it?"

The young bank runner mentioned news two years old which Manning had not seen while hiding in the safest locality for a fugitive – near the scene of his disgrace. After knowing police searched for him in Mexico he felt reasonably safe, but his isolation condemned him to years of believing himself hunted after the chase had ended. A copy of the ancient newspaper would have narrated what the scaler now told his friends. The president of the Union Bank had cared for him, educated him and made him a trusted employee side by side with his own son. This only and idolized son embezzled funds and managed to throw suspicion on his father's protégé. Briefly, Manning made no defense, was committed to the state penitentiary but escaped while employed as a trustee. Afterward he lived the uncertain life of a fugitive; but the state and country were not cobwebbed with telephones or provided with daily mail, so he succeeded in evading detectives sent on his trail. And for two years the hunt was abandoned. He was free to come and go like any other citizens and the thought of India deepened his gratitude.

To Franklin Manning was confided the delicate task of acquainting Jack Wylie with his real condition. It was becoming daily more difficult to answer Jack's questions. He could no longer be put off and it was imperative that his relatives be immediately notified that the boy was alive and well. This was the scaler's reason for being at the Brett home that particular evening and he began his probe with the query.

"How were you injured, Jack?"

"In our prep football match. It was going against us and I worked like mad. Once I pitched over a fellow's shoulder and lit on my head. An awful tunk. It must have scrapped my wits. I can't remember anything since even coming here. I don't know how the game scored and I'd give my head to know if our chaps won."

"Jack," said the tallier kindly, "you've been unconscious longer that you suspect. After that blow on the head you were irresponsible for – for months. You wandered far from home. You are two hundred miles from Detroit. Communicate with your people and when you like I'll take you back."

Jack stared at the speaker in incredulous horror.

"If that's true," he gasped," my mother must be frantic. Telegraph my father at once."

"That's why I'm here," said Manning. He placed a note book and pencil in the lad's hands. "Write your own message," he advised. "I'll dispatch it from town and bring you the answer."

As the nearest telegraph station was at Agache, Manning left Floyd to spend the time of his absence with the invalid and Phil while he used the manager's team for the trip. As he drove his relieved mind was busy with the fact of his freedom. Instead of bringing him disaster Jack Wylie's recovery unlocked his prison doors. He was at liberty to marry the woman he loved. Not for one moment did he regret his years of shame for his fugitive life had given him India. The two years he added to his bitter experience were splendidly rewarded. Without them he would never have met the peerless woman who was to be his wife.

This glad night of his release from fear of re-arrest was midsummer's triumph of rich foliage and gay coloring. At the Blair home Muskrat Lake spread before him like a shining mirror. The scene was one of perfect peace that harmonized with the tranquility in his thankful heart. India joined him at the lakeside gate as if she expected his coming and sprang to the seat at his side.

"Something good has happened," she guessed, meeting his glowing eyes. "What is it?"

"I'm cleared of the embezzlement charge," he told her. "For two years I've been flying from an apparition of my own invention instead of law-hounds. No one wanted me for any purpose except to receive the Governor's pardon, which is a statute conundrum. Why an innocent man must receive pardon instead of bestowing pardon is a legal mystery."

He told her the details of Jack Wylie's revelation.

India turned toward him dark eyes flooded with love and trust. "You know I'd have married you for all of the prison term – and waited. But you didn't confide in me. You made me suffer too."

Manning's encircling arm and their betrothal kiss was his plea for her forgiveness. They rode in companionable silence that accorded with the dreamy quiet of the young night. Then came Agache and the crowded store where the scaler dispatched Jack's message and they waited for the answer.

Ridman, as usual on Saturday night, was rushed by lumberjacks buying provisions and needed garments. With practiced dispatch he wrapped packages and tied them with twine he caught from a ball that unwound above his head in a steel basket for the purpose and while he worked at top speed his snapping, mirthful eyes studied India.

"What can I do for you, Miss Blair?" he questioned in the usual formula.

"Nothing tonight," she told him, but something in his keen gaze brought color in waves to her handsome face.

"Permit me to be the first to wish you joy," murmured the observant salesman, and offered her his hand in congratulation.

At the telegraph instrument Nordyke finally wrote out the words of Jack's answer as they clicked from the wire.

"Overjoyed. Mother can't wait. We come on the first train north.

HORACE H. WYLIE"

As the telegraph operator handed the sealed message to Manning his black eyes smoldered with hate. He knew this man was his mortal enemy and intended to prosecute him for instigating Brett's murder. His safety depended on the scaler's death and that agreeable event was assured. This time it would not be left to a hireling. On the strength of the old adage he'd see the job was well done by doing it himself. The revolver was loaded and ready. All he lacked was the opportunity and that was a matter of time.

Stimson, in turn, was observing the bookkeeper from under bushy brows as he lingered for his check. And his ratty, white-lashed eyes brimmed with a light that might well have made his employer tremble with terror. Certainly the bush-monkey served his master from no sentiment of devotion.

The memory if that homeward drive in the soft summer night with a full moon banding the lake in shimmering gold is sacred to the couple concerned. Never had the scaler's return from Agache required so much time. Never before had India lingered so long at the gate. When she finally joined her mother in the lamp lighted sitting room Mrs. Blair also read the secret guessed by Ridman.

"I went for a drive," explained her daughter.

"I saw you go," smiled her mother. Then, "My girl, my darling," she exclaimed, and the two were folded in a close embrace.

XX

A Gun Wedding

To Nordyke's disgust Sunday, when he was to keep his appointment with Lily May, was gray with storm clouds while muttering thunder reverberated among the hill ranges. Rain seemed imminent but he circled the lake and chose to make the trip on horseback.

"For the last time," he decided. "I'll talk with her today and manage to shut her pretty mouth. If she plays me false and sends her driveling mother that ends it. I'll do nothing. Nothing! Damn her innocent simplicity!"

Having arrived at the foot path leading through the woods to May's farm, he tied his horse in the underbrush and entered the forest. He followed the winding track to a glade roofed with a canopy of dark green foliage that he knew to be a favorite nook of Lily May's. The clean gray trunks of the trees were stately columns that suggested a leaf-carpeted temple of the Druids. But the only attendant in the sylvan tabernacle impatiently waited for the girl he was to meet and inwardly raged that he had been enticed to the distasteful conference. As he stood grudging the wasted minutes the glade suddenly filled with individuals who stepped to the front like actors on stage. At either side of Nordyke appeared two bare-throated, brawny men who carried rifles swung across their shoulders. They were Jim and Pete May, elder brothers of the girl he had cruelly wronged. Mrs. May, her florid face red from weeping, and her stern visaged husband silently took place at the rear. David Johnathan, the belligerent circuit rider, finally came forward leading Lily May.

The girl was clad in the white gown Madeline Brett had designed for the holiday ball; her frightened face was of the same marble hue and her sky-blue trusting eyes were wide with terror. The only touch of color about her was the gold of her magnificent hair since even her lips were drained of their crimson tint.

"What's the meaning of this farce?" blustered Nordyke.

"This," mildly explained David Johnathan, "is your wedding day. And I am about to perform the ceremony."

"You insolent fool," rasped the bookkeeper, "how dare you profane your office?" He would have struck the tranquil countenance confronting him but a double blast of musketry roared above the bridegroom's head. He felt the cold steel of crossed gun barrels at his back and knew they had been recharged by hands accustomed to loading for fleet game. They were ready for action.

Lily May, shaking with fright like a reed in the wind, was placed at Nordyke's right under Jim May's ready gun. Her yellow head scarcely reached the unwilling bridegroom's shoulder. Long lashes screened her downcast eyes and her nervous fingers clasped in tense fear.

"Join hands," directed David Johnathan as coolly as if the occasion was a church wedding.

"This is an outrage! I won't submit," snarled Nordyke, his face ashen with rage.

Instantly the gun at his left burst into a war-like crash accompanied by black smoke and the smell of burned powder, while the unhappy groom felt the jar of steel as the weapon recoiled. At his side the childish bride wept wildly with convulsive sobs.

"We'll omit the hand clasp," conceded the affable clergyman. "Nothing matters unless you make the fatal error of attempting to escape. In that case your blood would be on your head, my friend. No one under the circumstances would be called to account by a settlement jury. Settlement men are queer that way and they all know you. So be patient. The service is brief." He opened a book that he slipped from his pocket and began to read the marriage ritual while Nordyke gazed wildly to right and left. At last came the time honored question,

"Walter Nordyke, do you take this woman, Lily, to be your wedded wife?"

"This farce is illegal. I've been tricked," cried the bridegroom, white to the lips.

"Respond," commanded the circuit rider sternly. "Respond correctly in the affirmative – or be shot."

"I tell you this is no marriage. I won't be driven."

The angry words were drowned in the discharge of the gun at his right. Powder peppered his white face, his felt hat was neatly perforated by a bullet loaded for this climax.

"I do – I – I do," stuttered the terrified groom.

"Lily, do you take this man, Walter, to be your wedded husband?"

"Oh, I do, I do," sobbed Lily, and looked like the flower of her name drooping on a broken stem.

"I pronounce you man and wife," stated the circuit rider with steady, threatening eyes fixed on the enraged bookkeeper. "And whom God hath joined let no man put asunder."

Producing pen, ink and a legal marriage certificate partly filled out he dipped the pen and handed it to Nordyke.

"Sign here," he directed.

The bridegroom stubbornly drew back but the cold steel of rifle barrels urged his compliance. The paper that was to receive his signature was supported for his convenience – and the document's safety – on the book in the brawny hands of David Johnathan. He could not tear it in shreds, and the wily preacher might be supplied with other forms. The May boys waited. Jim was a crack shot. Pete could bring down a darting hawk. Yet towering rage made Nordyke hesitate. He was not altogether a coward. But force – the urge of booming guns sent his slim hand to the dotted line and his characteristic flowing script accompanied the martial salute of Lily Nordyke's wedding orchestra.

The gun wedding was over.

"Now go!" ordered the bride's father. "And if you either deny this marriage to Lil or try any of your devil's tricks my sons or I will give you the bullet along of the powder."

"This is no marriage," insisted Nordyke. "I was intimidated. That old devil of a preacher perjured himself –"

"Silence!" thundered the circuit rider with eyes ablaze. "Utter no blasphemy at your wedding, you traducer of women. And remember I shall insert notices of this marriage in papers of the state. As for perjury, if you deny the legality of my service a detailed, circumstantial account of the whole affair will be published. Go your way, consider and be wise."

With a malignant glance about the circle that rested longest on the broken lily of a bride, Nordyke retrieved his lead punctured hat, jammed it low over his eyes and departed. Once more astride his horse he turned east along the road traversed by Floyd on his way to inspect timber that was not for sale. He could not return to Agache until he was over the crest of his black rage. It would be torture to pass the home where dwelt India. Altogether his state of mind was not pleasant to contemplate.

"This ends my dream of the Blair beauty," he mused, "and I've lost her by my own damn foolishness. That white faced ninny is to her as a drop of dew to a diamond. If I can't have the jewel neither shall the man who signs a new title on his letter head. This marriage was comedy, but Mr. Franklin Manning – if that's his name – will figure as chief performer in the next act. He shall be Caesar after the dagger thrust, or Romeo after the poisoned draught." He smiled evilly at the thought, and continued his specious plans for an ideal future.

"After our two-named gallant is wiped out," he decided, "I'll collect my earnings," he smiled at the word, "and start a new business in some exceedingly distant and obscure corner of the earth."

He had reasoned from passion to peace, and was even civil to Stimson, who met him some distance further down the road. The tool was seeking his master so was not startled by his timely appearance.

"Think of the devil," said the swamper, "and you'll see his horns. I was going back to where I saw your horse tied in hopes to catch you for I've trailed the man you want ever since morning. Right now he's where you want him. He's over there in the woods surveying the east and south lines of the Blair tract. Tomorrow he starts for Detroit unless –"

Stimson's voice held a suggestion.

"Why didn't you go on, you fool, and get him?" demanded Nordyke, but his dark face lightened with evil joy.

"I'm unlucky," growled Stimson. "Nothing turns out right. So I didn't want to handle the job alone," he sullenly protested. "He's spry as a panther with the squint of a lynx. This time I didn't want no bungle so you can help do your dirty work."

"But the horse," objected the dismayed bookkeeper. "He's an advertisement. The sheriff could trail him from here to Agache. What can I do with the cursed brute?"

"Take the animal a half mile in the woods," suggested Stimson, "and tie him. You've got to risk something. I have. Twice I've put my neck in the noose and you'd been darned glad to pull it tight so's to shut my mouth. Now we'll play equal."

The partners carried out Stimson's plan and were gratified to note that no apparent spoor was left on the thick leaves. The unwelcome equine was at last concealed in thick undergrowth and the two hurried on with quick strides over fallen logs, across gullies straight to the locality of their unsuspecting victim. They said little on the march. Men intent on murder are not inclined to trivial conversation. Once Nordyke asked a question.

"How did you cross the lake?"

"Borrowed a boat."

"With what excuse?"

"Fishing," Stimson told him, and he showed him the reel of fish line protruding from his pocket.

After that brief exchange the two tramped on in silence. Nordyke was gloating over the accident that had given his enemy into his blood-thirsty hands at a time when he doubly craved balm for his outraged pride. Ever in mind as they traversed the uneven ground lingered two hate-inspiring scenes. First was the radiant face of India Blair as he had seen her last; next burned in his memory the late affair of his forced marriage. The two filled him with a reckless desire for vengeance when ordinarily he would have hesitated before joining in the overt act of manslaughter. Not from moral scruples but because he possessed a lively and intelligent fear of the law.

That Franklin Manning had given Nordyke this rare opportunity was entirely due to his concern about the Blair boundary lines. In the morning he intended to start for home to clear his record and decided to spend the hours that must elapse before he called on India that evening in her service. If Steel and Hawley, through a dishonest employee, had managed to secure a fraudulent survey he intended to prove the fact. And because he desired to be alone with his self-imposed task and thoughts of India he told no one of his design.

For hours he tramped through dense woods carefully running a direct line from a blazed tree

Munshaw had once pointed out as the original landmark. By means of a small compass he next moved west from the section corner. His line extended far into the Company's slashing and confirmed his suspicions; fully half the winter's cut had been on the reserved Blair tract. Again he sought the blazed tree and verified his first survey. By this time the sultry heat of a storm threatening day exhausted his energies and he gladly seated himself on a downfallen giant of the forest to rest and consider India's best method of righting her wrongs. Both the county surveyor and Nordyke would claim the trespass occurred through error. Nothing could be done except to force restitution, and restitution would wipe out the Blair debt. This at least was excellent reward for his arduous tramp through choppings and forest.

Having disposed of business matters he became profoundly absorbed in personal affairs. Would the state punish him for escaping jail now that his innocence was established? As he sat pondering this and other future possibilities the lowering sky was rent by heat lightening and the report lingered in muttered reverberations. At the same instant his arms were seized from behind while a strong fish line securely trussed his violently struggling form.

"You do too much day dreaming, Mrs. Forrest Mann," said Stimson's familiar voice. "First you lose your balance and fall off the pier and now you've dropped into a cattle hitch. I usta rope long horns, and as he"- nodding toward his accomplice – "wanted you took alive I tried my hand at it."

"Besides day dreaming," cut in Nordyke, "you prowl too much." He painstakingly spread his immaculate handkerchief on the log lately occupied by Manning and seated himself. "But for that pernicious habit Brett would be alive today. It don't pay to mind other people's business."

The bookkeeper deftly extracted a penknife from his vest pocket and proceeded to daintily manicure his finger nails, while from time to time he eyed his prostrate captive, and every look rewarded him for his late discomfiture.

Manning lay on the ground with Stimson's trolling line cutting his flesh, but making no sign of discomfort nor wasting strength in useless effort. He blamed himself bitterly for lack of discretion although his revolver was loaded and conveniently placed, yet at the supreme moment he had relaxed his vigilance.

That he was shortly to die a violent death he never doubted. But, lying in side with his eyes focused on the clean and friendly wilderness, he conceived a strange purpose. He determined to live his last moments with India Blair as far as will power and projected thought would permit. He would repeat the precious moment of the evening before. Every word, tone and gesture would be revived. He had been given his hour of bliss free from prison stigma, at liberty to marry. Now he must die content. The horror stricken expression faded from his countenance and gave place to softened lines but intense reflection. Inasmuch as it was possible in life his soul absented itself from the trussed body and he revived the golden moments of that night drive with his sweetheart. He felt her warm, clinging arms, her soft lips; he held her dear form in his embrace and imagined her as she, at that moment, doubtless awaited his coming.

"Listen," growled Nordyke with a vicious kick. "You act like one in a trance. Since I've taken the trouble of catching you alive for the purpose of a visit, I'd thank you to pay attention. You've kept mighty close watch of my game but you missed some points and I want you to understand them. There was the log-spiking for instance; well now you're going to hear the whole story. Afterward you're going to commit self-murder, you know. That revolver in your pocket will be fired at close range with your heart for a target; your right hand will grasp the handle; you will be artistically laid out as if you had fallen after the deed. That organ with which you cherish Blair of Blair's mill and her interests will cease to pump blood through your now vigorous system."

At the cowardly thrust Nordyke smiled with the insolent uplift to the corner of his mouth. He was enjoying himself hugely.

"I shall then make the final moves in this game," continued the bookkeeper. "First in order will be the foreclosure of the Blair mortgage and the consequent humbling of my lady's pride. As for this land survey and the timber steal you have uncovered why that's neither your business or mine. Steel, who is a brilliant limb of Satan, bribed the link-and-chain man to manage a false survey. He wished to lumber the land off last winter, but too many were prowling – you and Brett for example. But the foreclosure will cover anticipated ownership. Everything hinges on that. Log-spiking was to have turned the trick but it went too far and one of the devilish bolts killed Blair. After that Stimson got nervous, the fool, and I had to help. I was the man you disturbed that night in the cutter, damn you. We'd have wound up the rival mill in midwinter but for your infernal meddling. Brett suspected the truth and supposed Steel and Hawley were rascals; instead, Hawley is a psalm-singing saint with no more idea of business than a plaster image. Then Brett began to prowl same's you. He even tramped in snow to satisfy himself of this notorious timber steal" – Nordyke grinned – "so Stimson obliged to follow him and shoot him in the back. We'd have done the same by you but I wanted to talk things over. If that idiot of a bush-monkey hadn't made such a bungle of the burial Bob Stray, or whoever his is, would never have made his startling find; and that octoroon or Creole widow of his would have continued to think herself deserted."

"You should have helped me bury him," snapped Stimson. "I told you how it 'u'd be."

"Shut up," ordered Nordyke. "When you killed that man in Hartung's saloon you didn't need help."

"You've harped on that till I'm sick of it," said Stimson sullenly. "You're as deep in mud as I am in mire like I've told you. As for this job you'll do it yourself. I hain't no love for Steel and Hawley's scaler, but I'm done with killing."

"Are you?" smiled Nordyke. "Well, when I'm ready for your services you'll do as I say," blazed the bookkeeper. "Refuse and I'll send my first shot through your thick skull. Two bodies and two guns would explain both." The grim humor of the imagined situation pleased him. He laughed outright.

"I should think," suggested Stimson, turning inscrutable, deep-set eyes on his employer, "you'd be careful how you put notions in my head. My skull may be thick but it holds ideas."

"Why, you scoundrel," cried Nordyke, "do you think I'd trust you a rod? That's why I borrowed your gun. But I left you a fish line. I knew you understood catching suckers. Later I'll instruct you in target practice."

Manning still reclined with his face to the forest. His mind was a gallery of pleasant images. He paid no heed to the quarrel between the arch-villain and his tool. Incidentally he wondered when Stimson would be required to fire the fatal shot.

"Of what are you thinking?" Nordyke demanded, turning his attention again to his prisoner. "You look as if you'd called the jackpot and held four aces. But you haven't, not in this poker deal. You won the first two tricks, I admit. You stopped the spiking and you kept back the fire I had Stimson set. Only for you and Floyd the Blair buildings and lumber yard would have gone up in smoke. If you had drowned by the pier we'd have won. Again Stimson botched the job. He should have stunned you with a club. He's a chronic bungler, a devilish –"

Nordyke's accusation was never finished. There came a sharp retort. A revolver was fired at close range and the bookkeeper swayed gently; over his dark countenance spread an expression of intense astonishment. Then like a badly balanced manikin he toppled sideways and fell on the leaf strewn ground beyond the log and the sight of his securely bound prisoner.

Stimson, with smoking revolver in his hand, coolly watched his master's downfall. To the horrified captive he appeared utterly indifferent. His victim might easily have been a rabbit – or polecat. Presently he replaced his second gun in an inner pocket, then stooped and rifled his victim's purse. When he again stood upright he took one long, last look at the dead bookkeeper and remarked:

"That wan't no bungle, Mr. Nordyke!"

"As for you," he said, coming around the fallen tree to Manning's side, "I told him I wouldn't have your killing on my mind, and I said true. Him, I've carried a bullet for these many days; the deed is as innocent as shooting skunks. It was him or me and I've made sure it ain't me.

"No, I ain't going to kill you exactly," Stimson assured him. At that he drew more line from his coat and began to tie the helpless scaler by head and foot to the base of two saplings at a suitable distance. "But I'm a-going to leave you to die by yourself when you get good and ready."

"You fiend," Manning groaned, then was silent knowing words were useless. A minute later a gag deftly contrived from his handkerchief made speech impossible.

"I learnt that from the Apaches out west where I got handy with the cattle hitch. Now you take your time a-dying for nobody's going to come round and disturb you. Before hunters find your ant-eaten body I'll be where suspicion won't matter."

He next pulled a small oblong book from his side pocket and slipped it into the scaler's coat.

"Here's a little souvenir of the occasion," commented the murderer. "It's Mr. Brett's check book. I found it in his pocket when – you know – and as it wasn't no good to me, and as I was bound it shouldn't be no good to him," he said with a jerk of his thumb toward the corpse back of the log, "I had to keep it by me. It's his business notes and bank balance, and when you're found with it on you they'll think you killed him."

"You devil," Manning wanted to shout as the hideous depths of the swamper's malice was revealed, but the gag held.

"After two o'clock," Stimson said, consulting a large faced silver watch. "It won't do for me to stop here gassing, so good bye and a pleasant afternoon and evening to you."

With a leering grin and parting nod he strode toward the waiting horse in the distant forest and was gone.

Manning now had ample leisure to consider his terrible dilemma. Not only was he doomed to a lingering death, tortured by hunger, thirst and riotous insects, but after death his name was to be coupled with the murder of the late manager. Added to this horror he was ever conscious in his long vigil of that other presence beyond the fallen tree. In imagination he could see the dark, sinister face changing to the marbleized majesty of death. Ceaselessly and futilely he strained at the bonds while he speculated on the length of time he might exist. Again and again he cursed his reticence in not confiding to Floyd his mission. Would his friends institute a search? Or – a disquieting thought – would they think he had slipped off to Detroit in haste to clear his record. With loathing he thought of the easy prey he had twice become to his enemies. Long he watched the lowering sky, then the threatening tempest broke and the rain descended in torrents.

As the time dragged relentlessly, slowly no sound came to the captive's ears save the drip, drip, drip of moisture from the foliage above. Birds had hushed their songs, not a creature stirred.

Above the form of Nordyke drops gathered on the broad leaves of an overhanging oak and dropped one by one on the white upturned face like repentant tears. Through the lonely forest roared the muffled music of falling rain; in the distance rumbled the bass notes of muttering thunder. This was Nordyke's requiem, even as the crash of musketry had been his wedding orchestra.

XXI

A Telepathic Message

    India Blair spent that eventful Sunday in joyful anticipation of her lover's afternoon or evening call. She had awakened that morning elated with her new happiness and never had she been so critical of her beauty or difficult to please in the matter of dress. Each strand of her dark hair received extraordinary care until the shining mass crowned her royally, and her creamy gown was ornamented with a scarlet cluster of flowers from the garden. From morning to noon seemed ages, then another painstaking toilet followed with a fresh gathering of roses for her belt and hair. Finally she chose to await her lover's coming in the beach and stood in the same spot she occupied the previous evening when he arrived with his good news and ready words of endearment. Dark clouds piled westward and heat lightening danced in and out across the sky. She seated herself on a boulder to think of Manning and their bright future. Her busy mind became intensely occupied with thought. So profoundly absorbed did she become in her reverie that the man she lovingly imaged seemed actually in her presence.

Then gradually she experienced an indefinable sense of alarm and with amazement she realized <u>that she no longer expected her lover!</u> Within the hour she had looked forward to his coming with certainty. Now she felt equally certain that he could not come to her. She was oppressed, terrified. Her mind was seething with unaccountable dread that she could not analyze. Something was wrong. Starting to her feet she gazed down the road Manning would travel, but she knew her hope of seeing him was vain. The fact that she was disturbed by Manning's absence far beyond its import astonished her, but she did not attempt to reason. Later she believed her sweetheart communicated with her by the force of his agony and intense thought.

To talk with her mother of an ungrounded apprehension was not advisable, and to acquaint others of her disturbing thoughts would welcome laughter. After some moment's reflection she remembered one who would serve her without comment. To think was to act. She ordered Billy-boy and her carriage and started around the lake to the Indian camps. To seek Manning at the Brett cottage or his boarding place never occurred to her as worthy of trial. In either case he would have been with her at this hour. The Indian she sought was not at the camp but she met him coming from Agache a half mile beyond the reserve.

"Shawnoga," she hailed as the Indian approached. "I want you to find Mann, the scaler. I believe he's in trouble. Twice Stimson has tried to kill him. It was Stimson who threw him in the lake. That's why he had you teach him how to swim. Now I believe something worse had happened. Will you go?"

Shawnoga nodded. He was one of the Blair mill hands and admired his brave employer who had faced death to run the mill when men held back. It was the surest way to an Indian's respect. Manning had likewise won his profound regard during swimming lessons that cemented their friendship.

Now that India had put her terror into words, the words carried conviction to her own ears and heart.

"The scaler was not at Agache?" she half questioned, half asserted.

"All gone; Nordyke gone, Stimson gone, Mann gone," the Indian informed her and his statement unaccountably increased her fear to a frenzy of horror. The combination of names seemed significant.

"Find him," she cried. "Seek him everywhere. Something is wrong."

Shawnoga nodded acquiescence, but his coal black eyes lacked expression; his swarthy countenance was stolid. He asked but one question.

"Where Mann stay last night?"

"He and Floyd were with Bob Stray at the Brett home," she told him.

At the last word Shawnoga slipped by India's horse and started for Brett's in a direct line through the forest. From that moment India never doubted but that her copper-hued ally would accomplish the task she assigned him. He would find Manning – if not too late. He was doubly fitted for what he had to do as his quota of white blood rendered him resourceful, and his Indian strain endowed him with hound like power to trail man or beast.

Relief at having set in motion the means of assistance to her lover was inevitably followed by reaction. India began to doubt whether any necessity for such action existed. Manning would laugh at her foolish imaginings, but no other would learn of the incident. Shawnoga was too chary of speech to waste words. He accepted the errand as he would have carried out an order in her mill, and trouble himself not at all concerning its significance.

India's remaining afternoon was a time of impatience that sent her from room to room, and from indoors to the open air. Her mother believed India fretted at her sweetheart's delay, which was the truth; but she was certain Manning would come at dusk and escort India to the school house service conducted by David Johnathan. So she finally smiled being wise to the ways and moods of lovers.

Shawnoga speedily gained the Brett clearing and crossed the field to the kitchen door, where he knocked. It was opened by Aunt Sally who managed to interpret his query.

"Dat ar wil' man what de skuller goes round wid wants ter fin' out whar he be," she announced in the sitting-room.

"I don't know," declared Madeline Brett. "Neither did the manager. I remember Floyd asked the same question before he set out for Agache."

Without a word the Indian turned at the answer and started toward the barn. A glance in the stable showed him that Mann's driving horse was still in the stall. Sam, working at this chore of rubbing down the black's slim legs, turned sideways to stare at Shawnoga and exhibited much white in his distended eyeballs.

"Which way Mann go?" Shawnoga unsealed his lips to ask.

"Traipsin' round," declared Sam with mild irritability. "He done gone traipsin' off some' eres an' lef' me ter do his wuck."

"Which way?" insisted Shawnoga.

"Laws now, I dunno. Dat skuller's jes lak a flicker bird. He's here an' dere jes as de fit come. Don' ax me."

Again Shawnoga set out with no waste of time. His keen eyes inspected the ground for he knew Mann would visit his horse to see that it was fed before quitting the premises. In the deep, ungrassed soil about the stable was the print of a heavy boot he recognized as the size worn by the scaler. The track pointed toward the rear of the barn; at the east side of the building it again occurred and set off across a stubble field where Sam had raised a quantity of grain. Shawnoga needed no further evidence. The man he wanted had entered the east forest.

At the beginning of the woods' trail the Indian slowed his pace almost to a crawl. To any eye but that of an expert the human spoor ended, but Shawnoga was an expert. A dead leaf was disturbed in one place, a fern was crushed in another. Indications suggested that his man had turned southward by the winter camp and through the Company's chopping. In the labyrinth of tree tops and the piled waste of a winter's cut the Indian was at a complete stand. Vainly he worked in an increasing spiral and finally came out on the main road above Coon's farm.

Then the impeding storm burst into a blinding downpour. It made tracking even more difficult, but Shawnoga pressed on with his observant stare and presently he saw in the rapidly soaking highway the neat hoof print of the horse owned by Nordyke. A few rods further the track ended. Shawnoga retraced his way but only to satisfy himself that the hoof prints did not appear in the return trip home. They did not. The prints instead entirely disappeared. This interested the Indian. He became curious, but he was sure Nordyke and his steed had not ascended into the heavens so they must perforce have entered the forest. By this time the rain began to form rivulets in the wheel tracks and roar through the woods like a tropical flood. Dead leaves shone under the shower as if varnished and it flattened down such as had been disturbed, but Shawnoga circled and plunged into the thicket.

Before long he came to the spot where Nordyke's beast had been tied to a tree while his master departed inland. The earth, torn by impatient pawing and herbage cropped by the hungry animal, told Shawnoga that the beast had waited at least an hour. Careful investigation showed where the horse's trail led back to the main highway but the Indian painstakingly studied the ground to discover where Nordyke had spent that hour of absence.

Only the trained eye of an Indian hunter could have discerned the rain washed evidence of human presence. Rotten wood had been scraped from a log by a dragging foot; plants were crushed by careless tread; dead twigs were broken. To his surprise these signs were widespread. A boot-heel had crushed a squawberry vine, and near it a bunch of delicate Indian pipes had been crushed. Meager as were the indications they told him that, not one, but two men had passed this way and he dimly wondered if the scaler could be Nordyke's companion.

The torrential rain, coming twilight and scant foot marks now confused him. Several times he wandered but with dog patience he persisted until a deeply imbedded foot on bare ground set him right. But he was amazed to note that tracks were now made by feet that came and went. He had struck the boundary line paced off by Manning in his amateur survey. The scaler's vigorous stride had left abundant trace not effected by the downpour. Then near the northeast corner of the Blair tract Shawnoga's mission was fulfilled. His black eyes, peering in the gloom, saw two recumbent forms. One of these lay stiff and ashen in his last long sleep; the other, bound and gagged, stared hopelessly into the dripping forest.

"Cogago," the Indian uttered in the guttural noted of his race meaning "No good." With a bound he was at Manning's side where he knelt and cut the bonds with his hunting knife. In a moment the gag was removed and the captive, benumbed with his cramped position and the rain, struggled to his feet.

"Nishashin," the Indian next commented in his our tongue which interpreted meant he did not understand.

"It means you've saved my life," said Manning gratefully. He told his Indian friend a simply worded account of the day's tragedy while he flexed his legs to return the circulation. As he talked the Indian's face became expressionless. Since the mystery was solved he no longer wondered. What had passed did not concern him. Men had fought and one had been killed. It was all matter-of-fact, ordinary. More important now was his delayed meal after a long tramp. He was hungry and wished to promptly return to camp and eat.

"We'll summon men to remove the body," said Manning. "After that you may go."

Within the hour Nordyke's remains were temporarily removed to Jud Coon's log home. And shortly afterward Manning was listening to India's astounding impressions which had led to his speedy rescue. In turn she listened to the story of that murder in the woods – listened while her face blanched with horror and her form was encircled by strong arms of love.

At the hour of church-going sweet odors of rain washed foliage filled the air. The world seemed cleansed of both spiritual and physical vileness. It was tranquil, pure and inviting. The usual congregation ventured forth and for once virtue was rewarded for the little company was profoundly stirred by two astounding items of news. From his place behind the rude deal pulpit David Johnathan gravely announced the marriage that morning of Walter Nordyke and Lily May. His people heard the coupled names with amazement, but to doubt the statement would be to doubt the word of their circuit rider which would equal disbelief in scripture. In the estimation of the rugged populace Lily May had made a good match, had married far above her station in life, and she was envied.

But at the door after the service ended people were informed of the bridegroom's murder by Stimson and the latter's flight. Envy changed to pity for the girl-widow as excitement lightened dull faces at the recital of horror and low voices discussed the tidings.

Less than a mile away the childish bride sobbed out her grief in the privacy of her own room. Being dead the man became in her simple mind exalted. She believed he meant to be true; she was sure he'd have remained loyal without that hideous wedding. Hers were the only tears shed at Walter Nordyke's funeral; her bruised heart was the only one that remembered him in after years with love.

XXII

Frosted Cakes

Franklin Manning and Shawnoga were the chief witnesses at the Monday morning inquest, and this delayed the former's trip to his home city. Then the arrival of Jack Wylie's father – who came alone – brought intelligence that lessened the scaler's need of haste. Young Cutler still lived although reduced to a pitiful wreck, and his grateful parent used influence to secure the governor's pardon for both the fugitive and his son. Incidentally it was known that the banker had placed to Manning's credit an equal amount to that he had been accused of embezzling. It was balm to an uneasy conscience, restitution for years of wandering and a debt of gratitude.

Jack Wylie stared at the middle aged business man whom he joyfully greeted but with a puzzled brow.

"Why father," he marveled, "you look old. And I look old. We are Rip Van Winkle and son. What's the matter?"

"My boy," Mr. Wylie soberly answered, "you have indeed been a sort of Rip Van Winkle. It's all due to a blow you got on the head at that football game. You see it knocked memory out for a bit. Now we must hurry home. Your mother and sisters are counting the hours till we get there."

"But the game," cried Jack. "Who beat?"

"You had the ball," explained his parent. "That's how you got hurt. When you passed it to Tony Wyndham the game was yours. In the excitement you wandered away."

Jack's eyes sparkled. His enjoyment of that day's triumph had been long delayed.

"Bully!" he cried. "I'd do the Rip act again to win."

After Franklin Manning had taken Mr. Wylie and Jack to the Hickory Vale station he joined Floyd at Agache, where the manager was trying to straighten out the bookkeeper's accounts.

"Nordyke's books and private papers reveal enough chicanery to open Hawley's eyes. Hawley's a dreamer. I've long suspected that he was ignorant of business details. He moons over classics while Steel conducts business affairs. Steel and Nordyke were the real firm. I have come to an understanding with each partner by telegrams."

"How about the Blair debt and the timber steal?" asked Manning.

"One offsets the other. There's to be no prosecution. India is acting on my advice in the matter, and the settlement is hugely in her favor."

"What have you learned of Brett's affairs?"

"A Cleveland bank endorses the seven thousand dollar deposit jotted down in the book Stimson took from the body. As for the murder it is impossible to prove that Steel was an accessory, a master mind. We can only apprehend the tool – Stimson."

"Have you heard from the sheriff?" questioned Manning.

"He wired me that the murderer had slipped through their fingers. But he has help. The man was wanted in Illinois. They'll get him sooner or later. He'll pay the price."

Floyd was right. Stimson paid the penalty of his crimes, but he selected a doom not meted out by the law of either state. Shawnoga, crossing Muskrat Lake on the first weight-bearing ice of the succeeding winter, happened upon a sight that held him motionless. Under the new transparent covering, like a rare object under glass, the amazed Indian saw the ferret face and body of the fugitive.

"Nishashin," he muttered, and started at a lope for Agache and help.

"It's heem," attested Jules Deveraux when several lumberjacks reach the spot with axes and spades – the latter for internment. "It's tat wizzle, Stimson!"

It was Hilliker who searched the murderer's soaked clothing and, from a leather purse extracted a pencil-traced note which read,

"Thur hain't no place on top of earth for a man that is dogged by sheriffs from 2 states. I reckon the best thing for is a deth of my own choos. And for a rest spot I choos Muskrat lake.

Stimson"

Silently the lumberjacks buried the fugitive on a bleak spot of the north shore after simple preparations.

"He was a bad man all right," Hilliker thoughtfully remarked, "but Nordyke was worse."

"Most any man's character," spoke Ben Heald, "is like Guy's complexion; it's freckled. Some has more an' some has less, but all of 'em has spots."

"That's so, begob," agreed Munshaw. "Nobody made his skin, an mebby thot poor cuss was born wid a freckled soul. God rist him."

This was Stimson's burial service.

The story of Manning's self-sacrifice and his benefactor's grateful payment spread until every person in the settlement was familiar with the facts. Therefore when the scaler called at the Blair home India charged him with being the owner of undesired wealth.

"I thought I was to marry a penniless lumberjack," she complained, but with eyes dancing.

"So you shall," Manning promised. "After we use the money building a modern mill and buying timber the cash will be gone."

"But more coming," reminded India with a radiant smile. "I'm glad, glad, glad! A big mill with gang saws has been a dream of my life."

"And now that Hod Elwin has learned to scale, I'm going to set him at work while I visit Detroit and Jackson. There must be no mistake about making my peace with the state for jail-breaking."

India's happy face clouded.

"But when I return – the first of October – there's going to be an outdoor lumberjack wedding."

"In a grove," completed India. "And everybody shall come."

Consequently India Blair's wedding day dawned amid a riot of autumn color that flamed in scarlet or burst into a glory of gold, while the eternal green of pine or hemlock accented the brilliant hues. It was a setting exquisitely suited to the girl lumberjack who loved color and outdoor life.

For the occasion long tables were built under the spreading canopy of imprisoned sunshine, and for a week the Blair kitchen was a spirited scene of culinary operations, and at Madeline Brett's the same condition prevailed since Aunt Sally volunteered to lend much needed assistance. Sally was in the height of her glory, but Sam managed to usually be in the depth of despair. From morning to night he received a succession of orders impossible of execution because of their multiplicity.

"I ain' no hose, an' I ain' no centipede," he grumbled when sent to inspect hens' nests the seventh time for possible eggs. "W'en pusson on'y got one pair o' laigs yo' kain't mek 'em do wuk o' a hunnered laigs."

"Anyways, yo, gotter mek dem thutty hens do de wuk o' frostin' dese yere cakes. I ain' goin' to frost no cakes wid sto' eggs, min' dat!"

"What's the matter with the hens?" laughed a voice at the open door, and Mrs. Swisher edged inside the protecting screen and gaily flounced into the busy kitchen where Sally and her mistress were hard at work. "Aunt Sally is helping Deb Huff bake for the wedding," Madeline explained as she pushed forward the low rocker.

"Now why do you call her Aunt?" demanded Mrs. Swisher, intent upon exploding settlement prejudices.

"It's a southern custom, Madeline explained as she rapidly looked over glistening blackberries. "Sometimes I call her mammy. You know she was my nurse when I was a child."

"Oh!" ejaculated the caller. "Folks didn't understand. None of us has ever been south." She stored the item in her mind ready for the next quilting bee. Then and there she'd end the talk of Mrs. Brett having "nigger" blood.

"That wedding is the biggest thing ever happened in the settlement," she briskly commented. "Folks are going from all around. Every girl is making up new clothes to wear – except poor Lily Nordyke," she added in a lower tone of commiseration.

Sam, at that moment, reappeared outside the screen door. Like a dusky portrait, framed and covered, he stood anxious and deprecating.

"Dere ain' no mo' eggs," he reported from his safe vantage ground back of the screen. "But jes the same dere's a hen on, an' she's been on t'ree days. She's a settin' on dat nest yo' fixed an' she pears powerful uneasy. But she's a settin'."

"Course she's a settin'," snapped Sally. "She's been a settin' sence week fore last. I been a breakin' 'er up."

"How do you make hens stop setting?" Mrs. Swisher inquired with a view to collecting useful information.

'Jes' as easy," boasted Sally. "W'en a fool hen don' know nuff to quit settin' I fexes a slab o' ice outen de ice house in de bottom of 'er nest," she explained as she painstakingly smoothed the frosting on her last cake with a knife blade. "Hit sort o' cools dere setting instinct an' dey quits."

"I should think she would act uneasy," laughed Mrs. Swisher.

"Yes'm," Sally assured her, "dat hen tries settin' on de out edge twell her right foot's mos' froze; den she hists ober and sets de udder way 'round twell her left foot so col' she kaint stand it. If dat ice cake was a red hot griddle she couldn't mek mo' fuss."

The day of the great event dawned in a mellow flood of sunshine, while hills wore the blue October haze. It was a rare holiday for the settlement people who enjoyed few occasions of public interest. Early in the day farm wagons drawn by staid horses or moon-eyed oxen focused on country roads at the selected grove which formed a bower of brilliant tints while blue water sparkled westward for miles, and the Indian Queen puffed at her moorings, passenger laden and ready for brief excursions. White draped tables in hospitable rows promised the coming feast, and a huge cedar-walled bower gave forth the stirring strains of Jet Lowney's leading fiddle and Hod Elwin's stentorian dance call,
"First lady balance with the right hand gent; and swing with the girl behind you!"
Zoe Higbee, startlingly arrayed in plaid, cast possessive eyes at Matt Crane; but that vigorously dancing lumberjack saw no one all that day but quiet, gentle Em Jobbin.
Children swarmed everywhere, and silent groups of Indians stolidly watched the proceedings with Shawnoga as leader. At last Brinkley put his head inside the cedar bower and waved a signal to the orchestra.
"Hit up that march tune," he ordered. "The wedding folks are here and going on the stand. Be lively!"
Instantly the dancing stopped. The fiddlers stepped out in the open and faced the raised platform where the marriage ceremony was about to take place. Without a thought of its incongruity Jet Lowney struck

up the piercing strains of <u>Sherman in His March to the Sea</u> and Tom Bordon joined in with spirit while the bass viol droned pessimistic notes of Sherman's triumphant progress.

David Johnathan, with the same book in his hand he had used at the gun wedding, stepped to his place. Before him stood the athletic, distinguished figure of Franklin Manning, no longer a mystery but a trusted citizen; by his side was India, the girl lumberjack clad in white for the occasion but retaining her usual jaunty appearance, her vivid face radiant and her dark eyes glowing with happiness. Near the bride sat gentle Mrs. Blair, and at the rear in a soft creamy gown donned for India's wedding, stood the beautiful teacher of District Number Four acting as bridesmaid. Robert Floyd, now Hawley's resident partner in place of Steel who tactfully resigned, was Manning's honored best man. His strongly handsome face was often turned toward Madeline and his deep blue eyes noted the exquisite flush in her olive skin, the graceful lines of her beautiful form.

"She shall be mine," he mentally vowed, "to guard and cherish while life lasts;" and like an undertone to his thought sounded the closing words of the ceremony.

Instantly arose a deafening cheer from the assembled lumberjacks, and back of it Jet's orchestra broke into the strains of a favorite lumbering song which a hundred voices swelled to a mighty rhythm that filled the canopy of foliage and drifted to the Indian Queen on the lake;

"And once more a-lumbering go, and once more a-lumbering go,
We'll rove the wild woods over and once more a-lumbering go."

The End

Lightning Source UK Ltd.
Milton Keynes UK
UKHW03f1127010518
321931UK00001B/202/P